BOOK 1 OF THE SANCTUARY CHRONICLES

SHOTGUN FINISH

GREG RODE

ISBN: 978-1-7350915-4-9

Rode. Greg
Shotgun Finish

Edited by: Melissa Long
Illustrations by: Merissa Jones

Published by WARREN Publishing
Charlotte, NC
www.warrenpublishing.net
Printed in the United States

To my "Insiders," who have patiently come
along on this journey: Abby Rode, Dad, Eric Rode,
Frank Samra, Lara Eller, and Elisa Considine.

Part One: Foreplay

FIRST HOLE
Par 4, 300 yards

The first hole is a straight par 4, gently rising from the tee boxes to an elevated green with a small handful of sand traps that should be out of play unless you crush your tee shot and pull it left or hit a short shot and push right. A fairly generous first hole, though I can't see the flag. The plate in the ground reads 300 yards; I know which tee box I'm in, but the markers are scattered around helter-skelter. I can see engraved stones that read "MEMBER," "CHAMPION," and "DYE;" they're lying about like toys discarded by a child with a short attention span.

Dye, ha ha. A famous course designer, now very apropos.

Thankfully, there is nothing to worry about as far as where to hit from—there are no starters, no gallery waiting for me to hit my shot as I worry about my typical slice. I'm out here alone. I hope.

It's completely silent as I push a tee and ball into the spongy turf. No mowers or other yard tools with suburban dads at the helm, grinding their way away in the background; no children yelling as they play—games we've been playing for generations, which have now gone the way of the dinosaurs. The constant hum of golf carts, the *clink-thwack* from the driving range, and the mutter of men enjoying the outdoors is all gone.

I'd gotten pretty loose on the range. With the few dozen balls I could find, I worked a winter's worth of protesting muscles into some semblance of my old swing. I mostly spent the cold months indoors, working out and preparing my physical self. I recently added ten pounds of additional muscle mass. That's likely not helpful when holding a golf club, but I have my reasons. My mental condition might be another story after a too-quiet winter, but it's good to be outside doing something normal.

I scan the fairway and rough on either side and see nothing of concern before I step closer for a practice swing. Every shot, every round, I take a full practice swing. It's more for the moment of peace and concentration before striking the ball, but I'm not a particularly good golfer, so the extra swing never seems to hurt. I walk closer to the ball, address it, and look down the fairway. I then see what might be the corner of a golf cart tucked up on the right of the rough, under a river birch that leans over the fairway from a small hillock, protecting the green from errant tee shots with a side of slice. Like mine—I know that tree well. Regardless, the cart is likely out of my reach and hasn't moved. There might or might not be someone in the cart, but there is a splash of red visible. I can't tell for sure, and I'm not going to check unless my ball lands nearby. Even then, I might allow myself a mulligan if it does—no one will know.

I'm hitting driver here since I'm no driving-range hero and will never hit the ball 300 yards, especially not uphill. The driver is brand new. On my way to the range, I'd peeled the cellophane and price tag off and let them flutter away in the light, spring breeze. Even though it's last year's model, it's still stickered at $299.99.

Not surprisingly, there had been no one in the pro shop, so I just helped myself and left a note on the counter. I picked up a few sleeves of balls, a hat, and some sunscreen as well.

The driver is a balanced work of art, with a white body and black face. The display had promised between twenty to thirty yards of additional distance, better control and lower scores. Who knows, it might even make my dick bigger too. It's practically a weapon, harkening back to the days when men settled their differences with other clubs. It whispers through the air as I follow through, stirring some loose grass pieces as it reaches the bottom of my swing.

One more practice swing for luck.

Also, I want to get used to the feel of the .45 handgun tucked into the waistband of my pants at my lower back. I'd considered the revolver, but the bulk of the chamber might be (more) distracting than the flatter automatic. The additional rounds in the clip may come in handy too. My golfing shouldn't be too bad with the gun, but I'll consider putting it down on the ground depending on how the round goes.

One last look around.

My car and the sounds of my range time may have gotten some attention from the new neighbors, but for now there is no one in sight.

Keeping my head steady, left arm straight and eyes on the ball, I swing. It's a clean shot, and as I turn through, I pick up the flight of the ball, which is howling down the fairway at a fairly low trajectory compared to my old shots. Buddies have joked that the local airport alters flight patterns on the days I play since even my 4-iron flies high enough to knock down an airplane.

The ball lands well beyond and just left of the 150-yard stake, rolling up to the base of the raised green and trickling off to the right. By my guess, I just hit it close to 280 yards, so at least for now, I'm going to keep the driver. Booyah.

Hoisting the overheavy bag onto my shoulders, I begin to walk up the fairway. No carts available today. I don't have extra clubs in my bag or anything, but the other extras I had to bring with me are heavy. The position of the bag causes the handgun to dig into my back, so I shift the gun around to the front. It's at least a little less uncomfortable considering where the barrel is now pointing. I haven't walked eighteen holes since I was in my early twenties, so we'll see how this goes, especially with the extra weight. It's a gorgeous, early spring day, clear skies and about seventy degrees with low humidity. The grass in the fairway is a smidge longer than the greenskeepers are likely to prefer, but not much is to be done about that.

I reach my ball and put my bag down, picking out my sand wedge for the next shot. Before swinging, I walk up to the level of the green to see where the hole is. I find it in the back right with the flagstick laying flat beside it on the green. I put it back in the hole and return to my ball, my eyes continually scanning my surroundings for anything of concern. Golf can be tricky enough without feeling like I'm looking over my shoulder all the time. Nothing in sight other than grass and trees, which is good by me. As I'm lining the shot up, I aim left of the hole and short since the hole is well back of middle, and short will leave me with an uphill putt, which is my preference. *Click* goes the shot, and the ball arcs softly through the air, lands with a mild thump, and then trickles to within eight feet of the cup.

I slide the bag onto just one shoulder for the move forward and exchange sand wedge for putter as I'm walking. I pause at the ball mark I've left, pondering whether it makes any difference if I repair it or not. Old habit wins out—you always repair your ball marks; that's strict golf etiquette. I stop, dig a repair tool out of my bag, and gently restore the flaw in the surface of the otherwise pristine green.

The flagstick drops to the ground with a rattling slap. It's a pretty simple putt; I see no real break other than half a ball from left to right, and it's maybe a three- or four-inch incline. For a change, I hit the ball smoothly, keep my head down, and the ball drops right in the middle of the cup for a birdie.

I'll be damned. I should go home right now since it's not likely to get any better than this.

One under par.

SECOND HOLE:
Par 4, 327 yards

The tee box for the second hole is much higher in elevation than the first hole. I've got a commanding view of the neighborhood, driving range, and main road into the development. I take out my binoculars and scan the perimeter of the hole, as there are houses on the north side with mature trees and shrubs providing more hiding places than the last hole. The biggest thing to be on alert for is how quiet my new neighbors can be. They don't seem intelligent, or particularly fast, but they can be fairly stealthy. My guess is that it's not by design, just "being lucky."

Seeing nothing, I tee up and go through my practice routine, which now includes keeping the .45 at the small of my back. Like lots of golfers, I'm fairly superstitious. So if it worked before, don't mess with it. That's why I like to keep two extra balls in my left pocket, tees and the repair tool in my right pocket, and my ball marker on the right side of my hat. Even though I'm playing alone, I still have the magnetic marker and clip in its rightful place—all part of my routine.

This time, the tee shot isn't as good. The hole slopes downhill, and according to the stone marker, is 327 yards. Perhaps my newfound confidence is premature since I've pushed the shot slightly to the right and off the fairway—though with super distance again. I'm enjoying this club and would love to compliment the manufacturer if they're listening. I know that every shot I've ever hit awry has been the fault of the operator and not the equipment.

I keep my head on a swivel as I walk at an even pace down the cart path. I'm not in a rush and would like to conserve energy so I can complete the full round. The bag is heavy— probably fifty pounds with the extras—and even though this is a downhill walk, I'm conscious of the weight. My ball is nestled down in the rough, which like the fairways, is longer than it would normally be. I'm lucky to have found it since it's one of those lies where you almost have to step on the ball to locate it.

That's one of those golf terms that never made much sense. A good lie is a ball you can easily see and find. A bad lie is this one—nestled down into the rough and trickier to find. Then, there are the piles of bullshit lies that get shared in the clubhouse over beers afterward about how far you hit the ball off the tee or the length of the putt you sunk. At least that step will get skipped today.

I'm inside the 150-stick and about thirty yards right of the flag, and I'm guessing roughly ninety yards. I have a GPS unit, but there is no signal. No surprise. Ninety yards is a tough distance for me with the pitching wedge since it's too long for my sand or A-wedge. Regardless, I take the pitching wedge and knock the ball just a yard or two short of the green. I'll have an uphill putt over a ridge that runs the entire width of the green, at least fifty feet. Normally I'd use the sand wedge here, but I have been meaning to practice putting from the edges of greens for a while. This time, the gods of golf chuckle, and I three-putt for a bogey.

As I pull my ball out of the cup and drop the flagstick in, I think I hear a faint rustle in some of the leftover, fall leaves. Looking up and all around, I see nothing, but my senses are now on high alert.

Even par.

THIRD HOLE
Par 4, 346 yards

This hole is where the course starts to show some of its teeth. It's a dogleg left—turning downhill left as well—with the green protected up front by a murky stream that slithers its way across the front of a vertical wall of railroad ties. Nothing too fancy required off the tee; maybe 200 yards minimum is fine to get to the top of a hill in the fairway and allow the ball to roll, leaving a (careful) short iron into the green. I pull the club head cover off my 4.5-wood, take a practice swing, and then hit my shot. The ball flies higher than it did with the driver—which is fine— and lands over the crest of the hill with a draw starting to bite at the end before it falls out of my line of sight.

The fairway is flanked by some thicker trees, and I hear some rustling at the edges of the north side of the hole. Reaching around, I carefully pull the .45 out and hold it with both hands, barrel down in front of me as I slowly scan the area for the source of the noise. From my peripheral vision, I catch some movement and turn quickly toward it. My heart rate is skipping up a notch, and I'm holding my breath. It's a friggin' squirrel, dancing its way hither and yon among the leaves. It stops as it sees me, nose and tail twitching as it tests the air.

I let my breath out and tuck the gun back into my pants and move along to find my ball. This time, it's sitting up nicely about 125 yards out on a slight downhill lie. This is 9-iron territory, especially since the pin is in the front.

I'll have to think about this a bit.

The pins are always going to be in the same spot unless I decide to do something about them. Maybe I'll put them all in easy locations so I can drop my handicap. No one will notice or care.

Another good swing, and the ball thumps onto the green, rolling out to pin high but fifteen feet or so to the right. I work my way down to the green, miss the first putt by a couple feet but drop the comebacker in the center of the cup.

Still even par.

FOURTH HOLE:
Par 4, 405 yards

Four hundred and five yards, my ass.

This hole plays like a par 5 since it's all uphill and has the devil's playground of a green. You can forget it if you are high right at the green, and the pin is down on the left. All downhill on the green from right to left—significantly downhill—to the point where it's virtually impossible for the ball to stop.

I hate this fucking hole sometimes. The flag is down so I can't tell where the cup is from the tee box, but it doesn't matter from down here, only for the second shot. Anyway, after another solid tee shot—I am digging this driver—I hack and chop my way to an annoying six, which proves that the hole feels the same about me. I notice the breeze is picking up, with some gray, shapeless clouds out on the edge of the horizon. At least the next hole is a par 3.

Plus two.

FIFTH HOLE:
Par 3, 130 yards

One of the easier holes on the course, with a mammoth green. The pin is right smack in the middle; the only risk here is hitting long off the tee and having the ball roll off the back toward the restroom building. This is 9-iron off the tee despite the distance and I hit it smooth and high—surprise! It lands ten feet from the pin. The couple months of layoff haven't made an utter disaster of my game after all.

I march right down the fairway to the green and realize I've got to take a leak. The restroom will be handy after I finish the hole. Not that anyone would notice or care if I just drop my drawers right here, but I'm sure there is *someone* around.

My putt is better, grazing the left edge of the hole, swinging a third of the way around before coasting to a stop four inches out. A tap-in par. I'm feeling pretty good so far. I'm pleased with the idea to change up what has been a series of monotonous days, and months for that matter.

Half-grinning, I make my way over to the restrooms, drop my bag, push the door open from its resting place against the jamb, and step inside. I quickly realize I've made my first mistake.

The bathrooms have no windows, and with the power out, all I have for light is the sliver of sunlight coming from underneath the edge of the door. I know where everything is though, but I'm almost immediately paralyzed by the smell. I've never been to an abattoir, but I imagine this is pretty damn close. It's horrible; my nose and eyes burn with the meaty, dead, rotten reek. I turn and fumble to find the small latch, trying desperately to escape the horrid odor, when my foot bumps into something soft and yielding. I stifle an unmanly squeak, rattle my way out of the bathroom, and stagger away from the door. As I glance over my shoulder, unable to keep myself from looking, I see an arm strewn across the side of the room, and then the door's return spring forces it to close with a solid bang. I turn, trying not to puke, and spin right into the arms of the first zombie.

Its breath is a match for the disaster in the bathroom. The only sound I've heard them make is a drawn-out *Muuuuuuuhhhhh!* when they're about to eat something, which is what this one groans as his—I think it's a man, but I'm not exactly going to check right this second—arms begin to close around me, and his face lunges in for lunch. Between the cloying stench from the bathroom and from whatever the fuck was recently in his mouth—*perhaps the mess in the bathroom*, my panicked mind manages to add to the magic of the moment—I can't stifle it any longer and puke right in his face. All of my breakfast lands with a splash and begins to dribble down onto what's left of his shirt. Somehow I notice he's got the remnants of a tie around his neck. He stands there stupidly for a second, apparently stunned. I stagger back out of reach of his arms, fumble for the handgun, and pause as his tongue begins to tentatively creep out of his mouth.

No. Fucking. Way. I am not going to watch this monster lick my puke off his face.

I take a deep breath, squeeze the trigger gently, and blow most of his head clean off, thereby ending the "lick the vomit" show. The now-real corpse totters for a second and then collapses with a thud.

Jesus.

Two over. One down.

DRIVING RANGE

It's the end of the world as we know it, and I don't feel fine. REM can go eat a bag of dicks, but then again, they're probably dead, too, since pretty much everyone apparently is.

It happened in the late fall of 2012. It came pretty damn fast, though I couldn't tell you what the source was. One minute, everything was "fine"—more commentary on that later—and then we all went down the proverbial toilet faster than my Challenger R/T goes from zero to sixty. It was all over the news. There were stories about a virus, people eating people, mass panic, evacuations, the Army being called out, chaotic battles in the streets, and then mankind's twenty-first century came to a screeching halt, and we went out with a whimper. No more internet, no more television, pretty much no more anything. I haven't seen a normal living person in months. Then again, winter did just end not too long ago, and even in North Carolina the winters are cold enough to make people want to stay indoors when the heat is off all the time. It's now April 2013.

The horrible thing about it was that it took no more than a week for the entire world to shut down. One moment, I was living in a thousand-home subdivision in a commuter town outside of Charlotte with thousands of other people and families, and the next I knew I was using a shotgun to fend off cannibalistic critters intent on devouring my brain on my front lawn. I used to spend my days playing golf, mowing the lawn, cooking on the grill, drinking with an assortment of friends, and now I occupy my time by shooting dead people.

Thank God they don't moan stupid shit like "Brains. *Brains!*"

On the bright side, since most of the mess settled down, it's eerily quiet as there don't seem to be too many zombies left either. My guess is there is some Darwinism at work among them too. I don't think they eat each other, though I can't be sure on that score. Based on what I've seen of their behavior, I bet a bunch of them froze to death in the winter months without shelter. They don't particularly seem to be any smarter or faster than a normal human being. They're also not hyperaggressive like the ones from various, old zombie movies. For the most part, they're shambling, stumbling eating machines who don't seem to be choosy about what they eat as long as it's meat. The virus seems to only impact the human race. Over the months, I've seen a ton of both domestic and wild animals all over the neighborhood and on the roads when I'm driving, some of them followed by a pack of zombies like the paparazzi chasing a Kardashian—by the way, I don't miss the Kardashians. I've also seen now-wild dogs going after zombies, so it seems like all's fair in the new reality.

The first thing I did once things settled down was move. My house was fine, but it was kind of in the middle of things, and it made sense to make some changes. "Shopping" within the neighborhood was fascinating. There were open houses everywhere, though some either had moldering and deceased prior inhabitants—ones who were *dead* dead—or damn zombies wandering around indoors, trying to find their way out.

More than half of the houses I visited had one or more bodies inside, many with the family in a single room in a sad and silent eternal embrace. I moved out of those houses quickly once I'd searched them for anything helpful or useful. There were some homes with a frightful mess inside, too, where the resident duked it out with a zombie. Whether they lost or won, I couldn't tell. The carnage was usually about the same regardless of the victor. I searched them in a hurry, too, since the odor did not improve with time.

I finally chose a house at the end of a street. It's at the highest elevation in the neighborhood, so I have a clear line of sight in most directions. It's on the smaller side relative to the rest of the neighborhood, with good windows and a large patio. The garage is big, too, which helps for my various projects. It also has a wood-burning fireplace.

Funny how square footage, the number of bathrooms, stainless steel appliances, and granite countertops become significantly less important when Armageddon rolls around.

Mostly what I'm gathering from vacant houses are weapons, canned food, tools, and propane tanks. I've got a few very, *very* nice grills on the back patio and dozens of propane tanks for cooking the canned food. All the fresh food in the stores went, of course, almost immediately bad, so I have eaten nothing but canned food for months. You know what scares me? Spam and Vienna sausages. Not internet spam—don't miss that at all—but Spam. I've looked at the expiration dates on all the food I've gathered, and from what I can tell, Spam, the cockroaches, and I are gonna last the longest. I am literally eating my way through the calendar when it comes to canned food, consuming the stuff with the nearest expiration date first. In about two years, I'm going to be eating Spam, Vienna sausages, sardines, and peanut butter.

I might have to shoot myself first. I'm not even kidding.

I'm surprised how many weapons I've been able to gather. Chainsaws and axes were plentiful within the neighborhood, so I've got a significant stash of wood, though I've used a good bit of it during the winter months. Unfortunately, even a roaring fire doesn't do much to warm the house. Although, it does make it bearable at least. Wearing layers—like Mom always said—is important. In a morbid way, I'd been hoping a zombie would show up when I'd been using a chainsaw to cut down some trees. Not that I *like* to let them get quite that close. I don't know, the juvenile, formerly-video-game-playing side of me is curious.

Yeah, being alone all winter has been great for my psyche.

Next was transportation. The Challenger is a lovely beast dressed in black. The price of gas is now as damned as everything else, so I decided I would choose a fun car for drives. I figured out how to get gas from the underground tanks at gas stations, so I have no shortage of fuel for the car. I also found a huge, Ford pickup truck I liked a couple streets over. It has four-wheel drive, a winch, and an Urban Assault front bumper. I gladly helped myself. Just for kicks, I'd peeked my head into the empty house and yelled, "Anyone home? Anyone home that can speak? Moan if you're a zombie. Mind if I take your truck? Didn't think so, thanks."

Yes, I do talk to myself out loud from time to time, but I'm hoping to find someone else who will keep me company. Preferably someone who is still alive. I'm lonely. Really lonely. I spend too much time in my head. And sometimes, I wonder if my mind is a good place to be ...

The roads were clearer than I expected when I first started to drive around. Of course, it's not like people were just out and about, dropping dead of the virus or by being caught by a zombie. I think most people hid in their homes, either hoping it would all pass or hunkering down to die quietly.

I mostly use the truck to go on my shopping trips through each street and house. During some of my earliest jaunts out and about, I found myself following all the old rules. I'd stop at stop signs, use my turn signals, stop at now-dormant traffic lights, and look both ways. I even found myself waiting for a light to change, out of habit, even though the light was, of course, out. Heck, I even kept to the speed limit initially. Apparently, we like rules and routines more than we realize.

Now, however, I drive like a lunatic banshee, especially in the Challenger. It's a stick shift, 376-horsepower monster that howls like it's being chased by demons, or perhaps zombies. I passed on leather, but I did make sure to find one with an upgraded stereo since that's now my only source of music because the power is turned off. And, yes, I did cruise the streets with "All You Zombies" blaring through the speakers. There have been a few close calls where I'd come flying around a turn to find a critter in the road, but the big car handles better than you'd imagine, and I've been able to avoid a collision.

Well, I do have that one dent in the front right fender …

I've been on all the local roads and know which ones are clear of debris or dead cars. I have used the truck to push or tow those cars off the streets I drive on the most frequently. The interstates are particularly fun since I have multiple, wide-open lanes to myself for miles in every direction and can absolutely bomb down the road with the windows open, music hammering in concert with the exhaust, hair on fire at well over 100 miles an hour. It's a release of sorts to just get out there, and the adrenaline blast of taking the chance that no zombie or animal is going to stagger into my path is exhilarating and liberating. I cross lanes without signaling, throw trash out the window (just kidding, I don't litter- that's a shitty habit people had in the old days), drive past inert cop cars without fear of getting a speeding ticket, and generally have a wonderful time out on the open roads.

The corridor north of Charlotte is a series of used-to- be-small towns, so I've been exploring all around, looking for other people. I typically drive down the main roads and through larger subdivisions, honking the horn and hoping someone will come out. All I've gotten so far is the handful of dipshit zombies that have been dumb enough to walk into the street and charge the truck. When a 5000-pound truck meets a zombie at forty miles an hour, the truck wins every time. The zombie explodes like a rotten watermelon, which makes me go through a lot of wiper fluid. That, however, is also free like everything else, so I can deal with it.

That's a weird thing to get used to, though. Everything I used to worry about is now irrelevant—paying bills, saving for retirement, staying in shape, having job security, finding a girlfriend. No problem. Heat, food, survival, companionship—those are the new reality. I guess the finding-a-girlfriend part is still a thing, but I'd be happy just to have someone to talk to. I am an unashamed beggar at this point.

On the bright side, I have *tons* of food and water. Like I said, this is a huge neighborhood, and I've cleared out almost every house of its food. I have rooms full of cans—all organized into fruits, soups, veggies, and the ever-lurking Spam. Same for water—I have thousands of bottles of water in every brand and size possible. I found a lot of booze, too, and spent a couple weeks getting a little too drunk every day in misery. I quit that when I woke up from a blackout in the middle of the road with a zombie no more than ten feet from me. I somehow managed to run back to the house, the zombie shuffling behind me the whole way, with the image of two stumbling fools meandering down Geronimo Court flashing through my mind. The thought of being eaten alive will pretty much take care of any vice.

Speaking of vices, my discoveries within the neighborhood homes were not limited to the aforementioned food, water, guns, and tools. I also came across an astonishing amount of pot, drugs ranging from antidepressants to Viagra, pornography, and adult toys. I'm no saint, but some of the stuff I found I have no clue what you do with it or where you're supposed to put it. Apparently, I had a much racier gang of neighbors than I saw on the surface at the golf course, pool, and restaurant. The pot is tempting, but since it definitely dulls the edges, I haven't partaken.

Eventually, I'll run out of food and water, but based on the number of grocery stores nearby and the apparent lack of any other Walmart shoppers, I'm in good shape for about two to three years. In the meantime, I've got to get to the library and begin learning about sterilizing water, farming and preparing animals I've hunted and killed. Those can wait a bit, but they are on the list of things I need to do to survive.

Oh, I also have a pet. During one of my earliest drives, I came across a betta fish in a nearby house and decided to bring him home with me. He's going to be the fattest one of his kind since I can get three hundred pounds of food in a snap. His name? Sushi. Because you never know.

I had to build a large fence because while the zombies don't seem to actively hunt, they're attracted to cooking smells and things that smell like possible food sources. They seem to be able to smell me from several hundred yards away. However, that could also be related to the lack of running water and my dearth of showers over the past few months. I can smell me, too, and it's not pleasant.

Anyway, with the home improvement stores being well-stocked and my credit cards no longer being needed, I spent a few weeks running back and forth to get material for my fence, including quick-set concrete, a post-hole digger, hinges for the gate, and a hatchet to shape the spikes at the top. The end result is some kind of combination between a log fence and a rampart—a full-perimeter fence of vertical split-rail posts embedded in a concrete base and standing about eight feet high. Since the house sits up, I can see pretty clearly over the fence from every angle. There wasn't any need to build it higher. When I have uninvited visitors, they tend to bump into it, work their way around it to find an entrance, maybe shove themselves against a section to test its strength, and then, once they realize there's no way inside, they move along. I do, however, have savagely broken glass embedded at the top in a smear of construction adhesive—just in case I need to discourage any climbers.

So, shelter, food, water, transportation, protection? Check.

Back to the golf course.

SIXTH HOLE:
Par 5, 485 yards

It's a walk of several hundred yards from the fifth green to the sixth tee box, which gives me a few minutes to settle down. I have a little puke on my shirt I try to brush off carefully as I go. My hands are shaking, and my stomach is still a nervous mess. It's been quite a while since one of them came that close to me. I think I may have been taking them too lightly. He was quieter than they typically are until he "said" something and I have no idea how he got so close to me without me knowing. Most of the time, I've seen or heard them well ahead of time. I've had several amusing afternoons of target shooting from the porch, picking them off here and there as they cross the street—like the duck-shooting carnival games of yore.

I tee up my ball and step back, slowing down my breathing and tucking the .45 back into my pants. Predictably, my good luck is gone, and I drill my shot out of bounds to the right, into a backyard. Grumbling, I hoist the bag onto my shoulders and head toward the shot and find my ball a couple yards outside the white stakes. Figuring no PGA officials are watching, I tap the ball sideways back onto the course in the deep rough. I'm well over 250 yards out from the hole, but with a shitty—albeit improved—lie, so I hit 5-iron back toward the middle of the fairway. From there, I'm inside 100 yards, so it's pitching wedge, putter, and I'm off with another par. Anyone looking to assess a penalty stroke for the tee shot can bite me. Unless you're a zombie.

Two over.

SEVENTH HOLE:
Par 3, 158 yards

I have to hoof it up a hill to get to the seventh tee, which is significantly elevated above the giant, kidney-shaped green. I stop in a small stand of bamboo to take the overdue leak, contemplating whether I can come up with any uses for bamboo for home defense. Goodness knows that stuff grows fast and thick.

As I reach the tee box, I see three zombies down on the green. They're apparently chasing a squirrel of all things. Talk about an unfair fight. The zombies have no chance against a squirrel, do they? The squirrel zigzags across the green, dodging their awkwardly groping hands. I notice, though, that the zombies are keeping the poor animal contained between them and are closing in the open space. I can see the squirrel panicking and moving even more frantically. Suddenly, one of the zombies moves very quickly and manages to grab the squirrel's tail just as it tries to dodge. I can easily hear the victorious *Muuuuuuuhhhhh!* from where I'm standing as the zombie rips the struggling critter in half—blood and intestines spraying everywhere—and stuffs the front end in his mouth. Although I'm sure I'm too far away to hear it, I think I hear the crunch of the skull as the zombie's jaws close. I'm sickened and angry. Not that I'm overly fond of squirrels, but the mindless brutality of it just rubs me wrong.

It's time for the rifle, which I'm now glad I brought along even though it adds to the weight of the golf bag. I slip the sleek, black gun out of the bag, being mindful of the scope as I clear the top edge. Lying down on the edge of the tee box, I take careful aim through the sight at the squirrel killer, breathe out, and squeeze the trigger. His head vanishes in a cloud of red mist, and the body totters back to fall over the cup, still grasping the bits and pieces of squirrel.

Damn it! I'm gonna have to move him before I can finish the hole.

The other two zombies dive at the body, clawing the remnants of the squirrel out of the dead one's hands, and keep eating. Disgusted, I take aim at the female one on the left, aiming at her knees to see if I can spin her off the green and away from the cup. The last thing I want to do is putt through the gore of a pile of dead zombies. Golfing is tough enough as it is.

I miss her legs and blow her right breast clean off her body. Now that I'm looking, I notice she has huge boobs—well, technically, huge *boob* now. I can't help but laugh, having to steady my aim as I'm tittering. She looks up at me with clear anger on her face—still chewing on the dead squirrel, mind you, with a tuft of tail sticking out of her mouth—and starts to walk off the green toward the hill in front of me. Excellent! I let her clear the green and then put a shot right in the middle of her forehead. She's down and out.

The last zombie looks up at me too—showing his new red mustache of squirrel goo—then turns and walks off, heading toward the north of the green. He disappears into a small stand of evergreens. I debate whether I should try to take him down as well, but I figure it's a longer shot than I should try from here, especially given that I missed—sort of—the porn-star zombie at this distance. I have a ton of ammo at the house, but I only brought a limited supply with me so the bag wouldn't be too heavy. In addition to the rifle and handgun, I've got a pump-action shotgun loaded with alternating shot and slugs, a KNIFE—you know, like Crocodile Dundee would say, "a KNIFE"—and of course a bunch of golf clubs.

I hit 7-iron here since the pin is in the front of the green, so it'll play more like 145 yards. It lands just off the green and, luckily, away from the female, leaving me a putt from the fringe. I walk down toward the green, taking the small walking bridge across a murky stream as a shortcut. One of the turtles that's usually hanging around peers up at me from under some of the greenery at the edge of the water, then ducks his head and vanishes in a dusty swirl.

I've got to move the zombie blocking the cup, so I walk over and nudge him a few times with my putter to be on the safe side. This may be a smidge redundant considering he pretty much has no head. He doesn't move, so I hook my putter into his belt and drag him well away, trailing a slimy, red-infused path. Hopefully, it'll rain soon and rinse the remains off the green. I want to have a clean shot next time out.

My first putt is, unfortunately, going to be through the trail of goo. It's either that or I'm going to have to try a tricky chip over the mess. It's a downhill shot, so the ball is going to run. What the hell, I've got a gap wedge, and I don't want to have to clean any of that crap off the ball, which I'm pleased to not have lost thus far. I'll try the chip shot.

I'm not sure how the exposure works with the zombies. It could be if you touch their body fluids you can get it, or you might have to be bitten, not eaten. Of course, I'm not going to test either one of those theories if I can help it.

The chip is fine and clears the sludge, but the ball does run down past the cup by about fifteen feet. I miss the first putt and tap the second one in for bogey.

Three over, three down.

EIGHTH HOLE:
Par 5, 475 yards

Some people will say—well, not right now they won't—this is one of the easiest holes on the course since it's a reachable-in-two par 5. That, however, presupposes that you hit your damn tee shot straight. It's a straight hole but fairly tight for fairway, with a heavy line of trees on the left and a steep slope down to the fifteenth fairway on the right. As you might have guessed, I did not hit the fairway off the tee, but rather I pushed the ball off to the right. I'm sure it's trickled all the way down to the fifteenth.

Shouldering the bag, I stroll right down the middle and then branch off to look for the ball. As I drop the bag on top of the hill and pull my 5- and 7-irons out, I notice two zombies well off in the distant tree line behind the green walking slowly toward the north and the clubhouse. I'll have to be on alert for them when I get to the green.

Finding my ball right where I figured, I punch it back to the eighth fairway with the 7-iron and then trudge back up the hill. Not gonna lie, I'm a little winded. I don't get much chance to do cardio work in the new world since it's not like I'm going to grab the iPod and go out for a jog. I just can't run without music, and I'm not stupid enough to chance it even though I can charge the iPod in the Challenger. Since I've got my little compound of a yard, I do jog around the house from time to time, but it's a quarter-acre lot, so the view gets pretty boring rather quickly. Therefore, cardio has not been a high priority. Maybe I can dig up an old-school Walkman from one of the houses nearby and hope the CDs don't skip.

My ball is still around 160 yards out, so I hit it with my 6-iron. I've never been a long hitter. I've got the strength to be more aggressive with my swing, but I have never quite figured out how to use that strength *and* keep the ball straight, so I—try to—swing easily and smoothly. The ball goes left and bounces into the bunker protecting the green, which has a huge grass mound between the trap and the green. That's just great. This is a miserable sand shot since the green runs downhill from there, and of course, I can see the pin tucked up close to the mound.

I'm going to have a chat with the grounds crew about where they place the cups. Oh wait ...

I've got a fried-egg lie in the trap, which is lovely since I'm here in three and will have no chance for par unless I'm awfully lucky. Playing the ball back in my stance with the club face wide-open, I take a mighty swing, exploding sand into the air all around me, and take a nice follow-through. The ball goes ... two feet. Nice. I'm in the same place, now closer to the lip of the bunker and the mound. Another mighty swing, and this time, I skull the ball in a screaming line drive at the mound. However, it's got a ton of spin on it. It hits the side of the mound square and pops straight up in the air, landing on top of the mound and rolling out onto the green. Out of habit, I grab one of the rakes to repair my footprints and excavation work.

That's when I notice the hand. Just a hand—with a dry, ragged stub where it used to connect to an arm—lying palm-up like a panhandler beckoning for change. I stare at it for a minute, debating whether to flip it out of the trap. I just decide I'll not hit into that trap anymore.

Two putts, so another bogey. Crap. Four over par. Three down.

NINTH HOLE:
Par 4, 333 yards

Nine is a water hole: a pond sits immediately in front of the tee boxes and runs off to the left. It's no more than 120 yards to carry the water if you're straight off the tee—though more if you pull it left—so the water should not be in play. Every golfer, however, knows that a friggin' puddle the size of a dinner plate is in play in your subconscious. The green is a nasty one depending on where the pin is since the elevation change from the top—which is the size of a goddamn postage stamp—to the bottom is somewhere between eight and ten feet. You're usually faced with a severe uphill or downhill putt.

This time, I crush the drive long and straight, the cleanest shot I've hit all day. Like every golfer on the planet—oops, there I go again—I'd love to know exactly what I just did so I can do it again. That being said, I'll also take my blessings from the golf gods when they're being generous. I won't question them.

As I walk across the bridge that connects the tee boxes to the fairway, I notice a body facedown in the water lightly bumping against the pilings. There is an enormous fish—must be some kind of carp—nibbling away at the remnants of an ear. I turn away, but then I notice one of the arms is missing a hand. This must be the rest of the person from the trap at eight.

Hey! Need a hand? Something dark in the back of my mind chuckles deeply and slithers away.

What a drive! I'm maybe sixty yards out. I take my A-wedge since it's just right for sixty-yard shots. For a nice change, the pin is in a more forgiving spot, down low on the flatter section of the green. I hit the wedge just right too. The ball lands with a gentle thump and comes to a rest less than five feet from the cup. Maybe I can take back one of the bogeys here. I'm carrying the bag in my right hand rather than hoisting it onto my shoulder and the wedge in my left as I climb the small hill to the green, just passing a fairly deep bunker on the left.

Mistake number two.

A zombie literally seems to levitate out of the trap, moving far more quickly and smoothly than I've ever seen. I'm so shocked, I fall backward and get my leg tangled in the shoulder strap. I tumble over the bag and go down hard on my backside. The handgun is underneath me, my ankle is still tangled, and the fucking zombie is on me in a split second.

The only thing that saves me is the wedge. I get it across my chest and into the air with both hands right as the zombie lands on my body, his ravening mouth open and trying to take a chunk out of my face. A drop of something messy hangs on the edge of his lip and dangles over my face before letting go. I turn my head, and whatever it is lands on the side of my neck with a wet slap.

Muuuuuuuhhhhh!

Not so fast, motherfucker. I punch him on the side of the head, feeling my knuckles sink into his flesh. I've always thought the zombies were kind of soggy-looking and this is reinforcement. He falls off me, and I untangle my foot, scrambling to stand up. My inner golf pro would be disappointed with my form, but the results of my next swing are spectacular. I swing the A-wedge baseball-style and tear the zombie's lower jaw off. Gore drips from the torn muscles and tendons—drooping like red icicle Christmas decorations gone wrong—and I hear the jaw land with a splash in the pond nearby. He's still standing, however, so I wrap things up with the .45 at close range. He tips backward into the trap he rose from, landing with his arms thrown out to the side.

Well, what do you know, a sand angel.

I tuck the gun back in my waistband, walk over to the pond, and rinse the wedge off, trying hard not to look for the bottom half of his face. Then, I go back to the odds and ends pocket of my golf bag and fish out my red Sharpie. Drawing carefully on the back of the clubface, I write a capital "Z."

Right now, I'm four over, so I would really like the birdie to drop. My best front nine here has been a forty, and even though the handicap computer has gone the way of the dinosaurs too, and I'll never get to record this round for posterity, I'll feel good at least. Taking an extra minute to slow down, I line up the putt and am just about to hit it when the gooey shit that fell onto my neck—and which I'd obviously forgotten—slips and falls downward, slithering its way inside my shirt. It gives me a wicked case of the willies, and I drop the putter like a hot potato and shrug out of my shirt as fast as I can. The goop flings out and flops with a soft thump on the edge of the green. I don't want to look at it—I really don't—but I do. It's a friggin' ear, or most of one. Jesus. On the brighter side, they don't seem to eat each other, so maybe there is someone else alive, albeit missing an ear.

I shout, "Hello! Can anyone hear me?" I stop for a second when the wicked, dark bastard in the back of my mind whispers, *If they don't have an ear, how can they hear you?* I hate that guy sometimes. All the time, actually.

I put my shirt back on and retrieve my putter. The putt is dead straight, and I manage to drop it right in the middle of the cup. Nice. Three over par through nine. And I've gotten rid of four zombies. I think that'll be my goal: more dead zombies than shots over par.

Wonder what I should call the zombie holes/score. Zogeys? DZs? I'm going to have to noodle on that one. Or putter that around in my mind. Or see if a little birdie can tell me. I'll be here all week, folks.

THE TURN

Like I said, I spent the winter months making the perimeter fence around the house, gathering supplies, and looking for other survivors—seems like pretty much everyone has been voted off the island, my friend. I've also gone through dozens of stores to gather supplies. I've got an incredible hand tool collection courtesy of the two home improvement stores nearby.

I've always been a reader, so I have also amassed a significant library of fiction. I need to get some books on survival and farming since I'm going to have to get around to that fairly soon. I made myself a nice set of bookcases over the winter, more for something to do than anything else since the days pass slowly, though hand-sawing all the lumber was a bit of a bitch.

I've told you about the weapons I'm carrying, and I've got a nice assortment of other pistols and rifles back at the house, along with mounds of ammo. There's even a nice katana sword in the umbrella stand inside the front door. And I've got a BB rifle with a scope. It's very accurate inside 100 yards, and it's rather amusing to lie on the roof of the

porch and plink away at zombies. They twitch like they've been bitten by a mosquito and not much else.

My first encounters with the zombies were much more difficult than they are now. Life hardly prepares us for killing other living—or whatever you'd consider it—creatures, aside from those who choose to hunt animals for sport. I'd never killed anything more significant than a snake in the yard, and even that wasn't much fun. But I think some of the ancient kill-or-be-killed programming is very much alive, just dormant.

The first run-in was at Home Depot of all places. I was gathering tools since most of the ones I owned previously were electric, so I needed to fill in the blanks with old-school hand tools. The aisles in the tool section were very tight compared to others in the stores. I was squatting and browsing through the chisels when I heard a noise.

A male zombie lurched around the corner and began slumping his way down the aisle, his shoulder brushing off the levels and air compressor hoses. At the time, I had already acquired the .45, so I shakily took it out and aimed it at him.

"Stop or I'll shoot!"

Really? That's what you said? To a zombie? Brilliant, my friend.

Of course, he kept on truckin', so I fired and missed, the bullet pinging off a shop vacuum display. I re-aimed, breathed in slowly, and gently squeezed the trigger. The bullet hit him square in the face, blowing whatever was left in his head in a ghastly spray all over the shop vac replacement filters. He went down in a quiet heap and was still.

I, of course, puked my guts out and stayed bent over, trying to catch my breath. This was when I learned, the hard way, that your head should be on a constant swivel in the new world.

Bachelor number two came behind me quickly and crashed into my side, knocking my gun loose, which slid under the nearby shelving units. The zombie was a spastic, gibbering mess, arms and legs flailing all over the place, with the cavern of his mouth trying to bite my face. I managed to kick him in the chest and skitter away backward, crab-style. I desperately looked for something to use as a weapon. I found a hammer/hatchet combo on the bottom row of the tool racks and grabbed it quickly, removing the leather sheath from the business end.

Not quite a Mexican standoff, since the zombie immediately rushed me again, howling and slobbering. I raised the hatchet and brought it down in the middle of his forehead with a gelatinous thud. The problem was, he didn't die right away but rather flopped around on the floor, clutching at his face and grabbing for my legs too. I panicked and brought the hammer side down on him, over and over, until he finally stopped moving. It occurred to me then that I could have simply walked away and left him to die, but panic definitely got in the way of reason. I was scared shitless at the thought of having to do this all the time.

From then on, I looked both ways all the time and tried to do as much zombie elimination as possible from a distance with the guns.

TENTH HOLE:
Par 4, 350 yards

Not much to report on this hole. It's a dogleg right, and you can't hit driver off the tee unless you can hit it around 300 yards in the air. I don't have that problem, though I consider it for a minute given the new driver's performance thus far. But then I decide I don't want to risk screwing up the round I have going. I tee off with my 4.5-wood, hit an 8-iron into the green, and two-putt for par. Sometimes the golf gods allow the game to be easy.

Three over, four down.

ELEVENTH HOLE:
Par 4, 392 yards

From here on out, the course tends to get rough. I usually shoot about five strokes higher on the back nine than the front, especially on the last four holes, which are a collective bitch. This hole isn't hard, per se, but it's one where you have to drill your tee shot in order to see the flag on your second, as there is a crest of a hill about 250 yards out. Then, the green is one of the smallest on the course for depth, running fairly narrow and perpendicular to the fairway. Long is jail, since there is a giant sand trap—I've decided to avoid all remaining traps where possible—and short leaves a tricky chip.

I'm off-tempo with the driver on this hole, hitting it well but with a leak to the right. My shot lands in a fairway bunker on the right edge of the course near the cart path, but it's probably farther than I've hit a ball off the tee on this hole.

If I could only hit it straight all the time, thinks the billionth golfer to have that original thought.

The bag's starting to feel progressively heavier since there is more of a change to the shape of the land over the last few holes, and the walk from nine to ten is at least a quarter of a mile hike uphill. Not bad, unless you're carrying fiftyish awkward extra pounds too.

This lie in the trap is a decent one. Remembering one of the few lessons I ever took, I choke down an inch, dig the feet in less than normal, quiet backswing without a big turn, and then strong swing down and follow through after picking the ball cleanly. I manage to do what I've been told and hit a not-so-bad shot, somewhat of a low line drive that runs 150 yards or so. That'll leave me in front of the green for a short chip.

I hit the chip nicely but miss the first putt by leaving it short. Bogey. So, now the score is even on both counts.

Four over, four down.

TWELFTH HOLE:
Par 5, 457 yards

Don't let the yardage fool you; this hole plays longer than that since there is a stream running at an angle around ninety yards from the pin, and the damn green is among the nastiest on the course. It's a kidney-shaped one, heavily sloped from back to front and also falling from left to right. The only "decent" pin placement is down low in the front, but you still have to contend with the slope. It is not a particularly large target either, so if you miss, you're dealing with a pond to the right and some foul pot bunkers on the left. Given the recent sand-trap adventures, I would like to avoid those for more than one reason. The worst place for the cup is up high where it's protected by the slope, the inside of the kidney curve—you literally cannot one-putt from low to high or vice versa—and the aforementioned bunkers. It's maybe, *maybe*, a fifteen-foot square target. Sadistic course-designing bastards.

Anyway, there is work to do before getting to the green, so I'm concentrating on a smooth tee shot as I take the long walk from the eleventh green, which takes me across a street—yes, I do look both ways before crossing—and then on a meandering path to the tee boxes. It's at that moment I hear the scream. A female scream.

I start to run, which is miserable with the golf bag slamming against my shoulders and back with the extra weight of the guns and ammo, not to mention mashing the .45 into my spine with every step. I feel like a gorilla running on its hind legs with another gorilla on its back.

As I get to the edge of the fairway and tee box area, I see someone running much farther down the fairway, perhaps 250 yards or so and downhill from me. It's a woman and hard to tell her age from here, but I can tell she has bright blonde, curly hair bouncing around her shoulders and she's slim. She's looking back over her shoulder as she reaches the edge of the rough, and I look in the same direction to see a pack of zombies chasing her. And not their usual shambling, staggering chasing either. They're pretty much at a jogging pace. It seems the rules are changing. I'm watching all this as I race to get closer to the tee boxes, which will give me a flat area and elevation to shoot from, *if* I can help. My heart is thudding in my chest like an '80s rap beat from the combination of exertion, nerves, and excitement of finding another living person—who also happens to be of the girl variety, which is not to be overlooked.

I throw down the bag, pull the rifle out, and flop onto the ground in the championship tee box. I pull the handgun out as well and lay it on the turf next to me in case things get close. As I'm lining up my shot on the zombie closest to the woman, I shout at the top of my lungs. The whole group pauses and turns toward me, and I pick off zombie one in a spectacular spray of blood from the head shot. The woman screams again.

"Up here!" I scream in reply, and she races my way. This creates a little bit of a problem since she's blocking some of the zombies, but I line the next one up in the sight and squeeze the trigger again. This shot hits one of them in the upper chest and spins him around and down. That might not have killed him, but at least he's down and out of the chase.

It looks like there are about nine or ten more in the pack chasing her, and while I've got more than enough ammo, I'm already afraid I won't have enough time to shoot them cleanly before they close in on her. For a second, as I'm taking my third shot, I consider grabbing the shotgun, KNIFE, and pistol and running down for a closer fight, but then I realize that would reduce my odds of survival. I might be lonely, but I'm also fond of staying alive.

They're about 175 yards away now and closing. The gap between the woman and the zombies is roughly ten yards, which isn't comforting since I'm going to have to be careful not to hit her—though, to be fair, I bet she's less comfy than I am. For now, the group is spread out a bit across the fairway, so I have lots of choices. Four of my next five shots find a squishy home in zombie bodies and heads. One of them takes a foot off, and the zombie manages a few, hopefully agonizing, steps on the stump before falling.

The woman is more clearly visible now, and I can see she's about my age, with a dirty, tear-streaked face and ragged clothes. She's running more slowly. The separation between her and the zombies is closing in a hurry. There are four of them left, and I have almost no room to miss her and hit them. Regardless, I line up carefully over her left shoulder, hoping and praying she doesn't change course. I squeeze the trigger again, aiming at the huge, male zombie closest to her.

She trips and falls. *No!* For a second, I think I shot her, but then I see that I've hit the critter I was aiming at—he's doubled over with his hands clutched to his midsection. Apparently, I managed to hit him in the stomach. The woman almost gets to her feet, clawing at the grass to get back up, when the last three zombies reach her.

It's 100 yards, and I'm not a pro football player, so it's going to take me more than ten seconds to reach them. Scooping up the .45, I leave everything else behind and haul ass down the fairway as fast as I can. The woman's shrieks are interspersed with the *Muuuuuuuhhhhh!* sounds from the zombies and I run faster, if that's possible. I can't take a shot from here for fear of hitting her, so I just run and run. As I close in on the pile of squirming limbs—she's alive if she's moving, I think—I just ram my shoulder into one of the zombies and flatten both of us into the lush grass. I spring to my feet, chest heaving, and put a shot through his nose, watching a funnel of gore explode from the back of his head. A second one turns toward me with a snarl, which is perfect since he's off the woman. I pull the trigger again.

Click.

Empty clip!

Without time to reload, I rear back my right foot and kick the zombie square in the balls. Somehow, I notice he feels as squishy there as the rest of them do, and my foot seems to sink in a bit. The zombie looks down and then at me, almost quizzically, as if asking, "What was the point of that?" Obviously, the old kick-the-dick trick is not going to work. He takes a step at me, but I bring the pistol down and mash his face into a gooey pulp, and he goes down. As I step over his body, I reach into my pocket for another clip for the handgun, and the screams from the woman come back into focus in my ears. Just as I slide the clip home and rack the slide, the downed zombie reaches up and tangles my feet. I go down in a tumble, face-first. I flip over fast and squeeze off a shot that cleanly removes the top three inches of his skull, from the eyebrows up.

Turning back over on my stomach, I see I have almost no shot. The woman is fending off the zombie with her forearm. She's pinned under the zombie's neck as his grasping mouth seeks her face. She's bleeding lightly from her hands and face and is struggling to keep him off. I lie flat, resting the gun in both hands on the ground and aim carefully. The shot is a good one—hard to really miss from ten feet—and the zombie flies off her body to the side and comes to a stuttering rest.

I slowly get to my feet, scanning the carnage all over the fairway to ensure none of the zombies are moving. I see the missing-a-foot zombie slowly crawling toward me, digging his ragged fingers into the zoysia as he pulls himself along.

Part of me wants to let him drag himself around out here until some of the wild dogs catch his scent, but I decide it's better to get it over with. I walk over and put a pistol shot in the back of his head.

"OhmygodthankyoutheyalmosthadmeandIwouldhavediediditwasn'tforyou" comes tumbling out of the woman's mouth as I walk back toward the tee box and my golf bag so I can reload. I stop to look at her. She's filthy, bloody—which makes me nervous—skinny, and beautiful. Her blonde hair is a rat's nest of tangles and is scattered around her head like a child's art project gone mad. Some of her clothing is torn and hanging in ragged strips from her shoulders. Her hands and face are a muddy mess. Underneath that, though, she has a very pretty face, and the *very* lonely part of me can't overlook her compact but very curvy figure, especially with her shirt halfway torn from her left shoulder, exposing a lacy, black bra only partly covering a generous breast. The dark voice in my mind reaches out with a clinging tentacle, taps me on the shoulder, and chuckles. *Remember the last boob you saw? You know, the one you blew to confetti?*

A person. A live person. A live, female person. A lovely-under-the-dirt, live, female person! I haven't spoken to anyone in months—let alone *touched* another human being—and I long to just run over and embrace her, for the comfort of a hug and for the death of an era.

But … the blood.

She comes closer, slipping her sleeves back down over her forearms. They must have gotten shoved up during her fight at the end. I see faint traces of blood dripping down to stop at her watch. One hand, probably both sub- and self-consciously, brushes her hair off her forehead and over her right ear, while the other shrugs a light jacket more closely around her torso, hiding the distracting—albeit lovely—boobie.

I lean down, pulling another clip for the handgun from my bag, and eject the partially spent one from the pistol. I slip the new one in and rack the slide so I'm ready in case there are more of them on the fringes of the hole. I have to know if she's been bitten and am afraid I already know the answer, but there is no other way about this. I haven't spoken yet, which I'm sure she thinks is strange, so I have to say something.

"Hi. You're welcome." My voice comes out in a rusty, unused croak and breaks during "welcome." I'm overcome by the idea of company of any kind and very overwhelmed by the idea of having a woman for company.

"What are you doing out here?" she asks.

"Just playing golf, shooting zombies. You know, typical Wednesday afternoon at the office." *You slick devil*, whispers my brain buddy.

She looks at me for a few moments, probably trying to decide if I'm sane or not, and probably, to some extent, whether I'm safe or not. She shrugs as if coming to a decision. I do have more guns than the zombies after all.

"Golf. Oh-kay. Can I come with you?" she asks. "I don't want to play, but I could sure use the company, especially company that doesn't want to eat me." As she finishes the sentence, I think I see a brief flutter of embarrassment cross her face. I guess those of us who are left are all lonely, but old rules of proper behavior apparently still apply. I let her comment slide without expression, as if I didn't notice.

"Sure. Of course you can. I'd like some company too. It's been a long time." My voice is unfamiliar. While I've talked to myself during these long months, it hasn't been very often and it hasn't been conversational. "Do me a favor, please," I ask, gesturing toward the fallen golf bag. Several clubs are strewn about the tee box where I dropped it in the rush to save her. "Can you toss those clubs back in the bag while I tee up?"

"Um, sure, yeah."

I think part of her is still a little thunderstruck that I'm out here just playing golf.

Or, you know, could be that five minutes ago she was sure she was going to die in a painful, nasty way.

I pull the driver out and walk past her so my back is to her and I slip the handgun into my waistband. By design, I lean forward on one leg to set the tee and ball in place so I can look back without being obvious. As she squats to collect the clubs, one of them is just out of her reach, so she stretches out her right arm to grab it. Her sleeve slides well up her forearm. I see it. A bite, fresh and bloody on the inside of her arm.

Shit. She has to go.

"Keep an eye on this, please. I have a tendency to get in trouble off this tee," I say, trying to keep my voice steady and light. I focus hard on my practice swing, blinking away the tear leaking from the corner of my left eye.

She walks forward and shields her eyes, the bag slung over her shoulder. She's a hair in front of the tee box and off to my left. My swing is not good, and I hook the shot to the left of the fairway and over the cart path. I don't think it's out of bounds, but it is near a dense cluster of cedars bordering the edge of the course and the overgrown yards beyond.

I reach for the bag, and she hands it over with some difficulty due to the weight. I hoist it onto my shoulders, and we step off down the fairway, not speaking. My mind is a riot of questions and sadness. *I know what has to happen, but I can't bear the thought.* I decide I'm not going to ask any of the questions except one.

"Did you get bit?" I ask as casually as possible.

"No, I think all this blood is from when you shot the one on top of me. They never got to me."

I know she's lying, and I can't blame her. I want her to not be bit probably as much as she wants to have not been bitten. We're both seeing our first person in months.

You cannot take the chance. You'll start to like her, and it will be worse with every passing moment.

I'm thinking furiously as we walk, wondering if there is any cure or if maybe she's immune since she's still alive after everything. There is no way to tell, and my heart aches in my chest. I'm crying openly now, but I don't want her to see it. I wipe my face on my sleeve like I'm clearing sweat off my brow.

We find the ball—luckily in bounds—but there is no chance I can try for the green in two. It's just as well since it's a risky shot even with the best of drives. Like I said, the green is sloped back to front as well as from left to right. So, if you don't hit the green squarely, the ball will trickle off and dribble into a pond. I've watched dozens of shots hit, roll, and then slowly make their inexorable way into the drink, some of them mine.

I play a 7-iron and top the shot a bit, hitting a worm-burner that still runs out about 120 yards and lands in the middle of the fairway, short of the green-protecting stream. This will allow me to go after the green with a very short iron, assuming I can get my shit together and concentrate again. Adrenaline is still firing through my body from the battle in the fairway, countered by my thoughts about this woman I desperately wish I could save and resignedly know I cannot.

As we get closer to the ball, I look up and around. The sun is shining, and I can hear a few birds tinkling their songs regardless of the disastrous end of the human race. The wind whispers through the early buds on the trees, gently swaying the branches and scattering some leftover dead leaves across the edge of the course in a delicate rustle. This section of the hole doesn't have any homes on it, just a stretch of woods bordering the fairway and rough. It's beautiful here.

Do the right thing.

As I address the ball, I take a slow, practice swing and then notice she's standing right behind me, which is distracting. Turning toward her to ask if she'd mind moving to the side, I see another zombie shuffling his way toward us from above us on the course, still fifty yards or so away and no immediate threat.

"Jesus, another one," I spit out.

She looks over her shoulder with a gasp and then turns fully as I'm hoisting the pistol out from the small of my back and thumbing the safety off.

I aim carefully up the course, squeeze the trigger gently, and the report from the gun seems louder than any shot I've fired today. The echo bounces back to me from the steep, wooded hillside beyond the green and cascades away.

The woman falls to the ground slightly sideways, slumping to the turf. I've shot her through the back, not wanting to make this any messier than I need to. The zombie must smell the blood since his pace accelerates into a shambling jog as he closes in.

Wiping the tears from my face, I squeeze the trigger again, knowing I'll probably miss. His right hand vanishes from his wrist. He stops and looks down at where his hand used to be. Now it's me jogging toward him, raising the pistol and firing as I trot, not caring whether I hit him. I need an outlet for the death of pretty much everyone, the loneliness, the danger and uncertainty of the last few months, and the raw, fresh anger over the fact that I've found and lost someone within the stretch of no more than ten minutes. This son of a bitch is "it." Months of sorrow and bitterness make their way down my arm to my index finger as I fire and fire. The fourth shot hits him squarely in the chest and drops him onto the 150-yard marker plate. I completely empty the magazine into his twitching body, screaming and crying until the third, dull click of the hammer.

I eject the spent magazine and slot a new one in as I'm walking back down the course. All the birds had stopped singing while I was shooting, but I hear a tentative whistle as I get close to the woman's body.

She's lying on her side, mostly face-down. Dropping to my knees, I turn her over, praying to whatever "God" let all of this happen, that she's dead because I'm not sure I could pull the trigger again. Mercifully, she is.

Brushing a stray fluff of hair from her face and over her ear, I'm reminded of the same gesture she made after the fight. I no longer notice her beauty, just my internal agony over what I, and the world, have become. I bend down and hoist her into my arms, stumbling a little from her weight and the weakness in my knees, and carry her over to the edge of the course to the last home adjacent to the fairway. There is a remnant of what must have been a gorgeous flower garden that has since gone to riot, but it will be a good spot.

I lay her down and then break into the house and go into the garage to find a shovel. I'm not going to leave her body exposed to the elements, critters, or my sight when I play again. If I play again. I dig a hole large enough and deep enough to hold her and then carefully lower her in.

Standing back up, I look at the sky and try to rediscover the beauty in the day but cannot. I drop to my hands and knees and lean down to her now-peaceful face.

If this were a movie moment, I'd be whispering something sweet in her ear, like "I'm sorry" or something along those lines. But this is my reality. I've been alone for the past few months—*maybe longer*, croaks the ever-present voice—in a goddamn zombie-infested apocalyptic world, and when I think I've finally found a person to spend my days with, I have to go and shoot her in the fucking back less than ten minutes after saving her life.

What's the real difference between them and me?

Burying her takes only a few minutes with the rich garden soil. I drop the shovel as I walk away.

Golf no longer seems important, but I've also always been someone who finishes what he starts, so I'm going to play the rest of this round. I know it would nag at me if I didn't, and I feel like I've got nothing to lose anyway. I might not ever play again, but we'll see what happens over time.

I'm about 110 yards out, which is 9-iron for me. The pin is thankfully in the front of the green, so I do have the slight slope behind it to protect me if I hit long. I skip the practice swing and just hit, no longer really caring what my score is. The ball arcs high into the sky—slightly eclipsing the sun for a heartbeat—right over the flag and falls with a thump about six feet beyond the cup. I stand and watch the ball, knowing it's going to move rather than sit on the slope, until it begins to come back.

I hoist the bag onto my shoulders and move to cross a footbridge over the stream, keeping an eye on the slowly moving ball the whole time. The golf gods are sick bastards with a venomous sense of humor, and the ball meanders down to the edge of the cup and stops right on the lip.

Of course it does.

I cross the bridge, keeping my head down to make sure none of the planks is loose, and turn slightly right toward the green. I'm placing my bag down on the green—not sure why I'm bothering to take my putter out for a shot that an ant fart would knock in—when the ball tips over and falls into the cup with a rattle.

Of course it does.

A birdie, eleven zombies, and a human. Three over, fifteen down.

THIRTEENTH HOLE:
Par 3, 130 yards

I've got to cross a raised causeway to get over to the tees. I try to use the time to clear my head. This is another water hole, except it's got nothing but tee boxes and the green. I imagine the bottom of the lake being literally covered with golf balls. I used to take a tired ball out for this tee shot just in case, but since all golf balls are now free, I play the same one. I'll take up scuba diving if I need to.

No danger here—my shot lands on the green about twenty-five feet from the cup. I'm getting tired, but I think most of it is emotional fatigue. As I walk back across the causeway, I'm listening to the hissing murmur of the pond flowing into a drain in the midst of the water—which subsequently carries down to the pond back on twelve—when I see the same old egret that's always there, sitting on the concrete frame and watching me pass. He's majestic in a way, proudly standing and staring at me with no fear in his unblinking eyes, which makes sense. There's nothing for him to worry about from me or my race, unless zombies can swim and like uncooked poultry. Who am I kidding? They like uncooked everything!

Two putts, par, and I'm hoofing it up the hill to the fourteenth tee.

Three over, fifteen down.

FOURTEENTH HOLE:
Par 4, 386 yards

This hole is actually close to my house, and for a few moments, I debate just trudging home and calling it a day. I can always walk over to get my car another time. I can't imagine a wilder swing of emotions over the last fifteen minutes—finding someone and then having to lose them, by my own hands no less. I guess it was better than not being able to save her from the zombies during the fight, but obviously the end result is the same. I'm still alone, except for my guilt.

Then again, I'm having a good round, both golf and zombie score, so I think I'll continue.

The tee boxes are elevated, providing a beautiful view across several fairways of the too-quiet neighborhood and the small pond at the end of a stream that winds its way through a number of holes. Again, I'm struck by the absence of background noise. This must be what it was like hundreds of years ago. If there is a God, I wonder what he—or she— thinks of all this. I doubt, however, that God has anything to do with the massive clusterfuck that just swept mankind aside like a child upending a table full of loose Legos.

Unless you go really far to the right here, it's hard to get in trouble off the tee. Quieting my mind, I focus on my practice swing and then absolutely murder the shot straight down the fairway. I like this driver. Maybe I should go back and pay for it. I wonder if they take plastic? No, wait, let's just put it on my member charge. Go ahead and add fifty dollars for yourself while you're at it. Ah, I'm a riot. I imagine the beer cart being driven by a scantily clad female zombie in sunglasses. The mind is a wonderful thing, unless perhaps you're alone after the apocalypse, like how I am now.

As I reholster the driver and shoulder the bag, I see a small group of zombies between the green on this hole and the following tee boxes for fifteen. They're working their way across the cart paths toward the clubhouse. They must be following something, maybe a deer or a dog. Anyway, they're 400 or 500 yards away. So, they're of no consequence.

My ball has come to a rest well inside the 100-yard stone plate embedded in the fairway, so I really mashed that tee shot. The only problem on this hole is that the ground inside 100 yards is usually soggy with either overwatering or poor drainage. I've chunked more shots in this area than anywhere else on the course, and I usually wind up with muddy shorts as a side benefit. Instead of hitting a close to full wedge, I decide to hit 8-iron with a short swing so I can really concentrate on good impact. The ball flies high, crossing the clouded sky, and drops just short of the green and coasts to a stop about twenty feet from the cup.

Two putts again, another par.
Three over, fifteen down.

FIFTEENTH HOLE:
Par 5, 514 yards

This is one of my least favorite holes on the course since it's tough and really depends on a good tee shot to set you up for making par. Forget birdie on this hole unless you can hit 300 yards gradually but steadily uphill off the tee and then hit a long fairway wood accurately into a green protected by a stream crossing the front of the green and a large tree that blocks the left side. Right. The eighth fairway is above this hole and plays in the opposite direction, so if you err to the right, you have a chance of the hillside giving you a break.

I bomb another tee shot, which I'm sure is going to set me up for making a stupid decision when I reach my ball. I really like this driver!

As I walk up toward my ball, my mind keeps flashing back to the fight and the woman. Was she bitten early on? Right at the end? When? If I had gotten there a little sooner, would it have made a difference? One more quick shot before a little nibble?

I resolve to begin looking house-to-house again throughout the neighborhood for other survivors since the brief meeting with the woman has made me realize how out-on-an-island I've been and how much I've missed people. There were times in the past when I was perfectly content in my own little world of relative solitude: going to work, coming home to a book, golfing, or watching a movie at home and then rinsing and repeating as necessary. Company would be really, really nice.

Up on the eighth fairway, I see another small pack of zombies heading in the same direction as the last group. I could probably pick a few of them off with the rifle from here, but my heart's not really in it at this point, nor do I want another direct fight with a group. My legs are getting heavier, the bag is dragging more firmly upon my shoulders—despite the ammo I've set free into zombie flesh—and I really just want to pretend I'm playing an ordinary round of spring golf.

It turns out I did hit the driver well enough to think about going for the green in two, but I don't want to screw up my otherwise excellent round. If I can keep this up, then I'll have my best score ever, which is par for the course—ha, I crack myself up—since no one is watching. Too bad Bill Murray wasn't around to caddy.

Rather than take a risk, I hit my 4-iron to just in front of the stream, drop the chip onto the green, and walk away with another par after my first putt just edges past the cup. Funny how golf can be easy when you hit the ball straight.

Three over, fifteen down.

SIXTEENTH HOLE:
Par 4, 369 yards

The final four holes on this course separate the men from the zombies for sure. I'd be cruising along with a solid round—not as good as this one, mind you—only to slip into a double-bogey rut on these last four and really spoil a good walk.

Here, you have to hit from a tee that's a bit lower than the fairway, which begins on a plateau around 150 yards or so out. From the tee to the fairway is just rough, but if you screw up your tee shot short, you're totally blind to the pin and have an uphill lie to steal all your distance. It's tough enough going into this green because you have to hit down to it from the fairway. This green is also protected on the left by a nearly vertical hill shored up by railroad ties that will dump your ball into the stream. Go long and you're on a bitch of a beach; go right and there's a valley that will slide the ball off the green. So, all you have to do is hit the right place on the green and stick the landing. Nothing to it.

Another superb tee shot. I'm just tickled by the distance and consistency I've had with this driver. Definitely my favorite new non-gunpowder-based weapon.

I'm not as lucky on my second shot, which lands short and in front of the raised green. It's the least bad place you can be, but the pin is way in the front, which is not good in this case. I've got to pop the ball up about fifteen feet in the air but less than fifteen feet horizontally. That's more finesse than I typically have with my sand wedge, and I'm not carrying a flop—those kind of scare me anyway. When I look at the openness of that club, I think I'm going to pop the ball up and hit myself in the face.

After a few practice swings, I hit for real and am a bit unsurprised to watch my club gouge the grass behind the ball, resulting in the horrifying one-foot shot. Every golfer, good or bad, has been there and has nightmares about that one. My second attempt is another familiar shot in that I hit it almost too cleanly this time, so the ball lands *just* at the top of the face of the hill, pauses to give a moment of false hope that gravity has stopped working, and then rolls back to my feet. With a sigh, I deposit the wedge back in the bag, haul out my .45, and take careful aim at the ball. *Ladies and gentlemen, it looks like he's forgoing iron on this shot and is thinking lead. He's only fifteen feet away and is bringing out the big gun. What could he be thinking?* Don't you love those guys? Half a mile away in a broadcast booth and they're telling us the pro is 162 yards out, hitting his 9-iron. Really? Like, *really?*

I put the gun back and take out my putter. I've seen other golfers do this from this spot, though I have always been too stubborn about getting the chip shot right to try putter. It works fine, running the ball up onto the green, but I'm now laying five and am eight feet away from the cup. My first putt misses short, so I get a tap-in triple. Just friggin' great.

Six over, fifteen down.

SEVENTEENTH HOLE:
Par 3, 141 yards

Seventeen is similar to thirteen. It's an over-the-water par 3 with nothing but splash between the tee boxes and the green. Depending on where the flagstick is, I hit either 7- or 6-iron here since there is a respectable ridge across the green that protects a flag in the back rather well. Just two holes to go, but I've got to bear down to fix the debacle on sixteen.

Goddamn tee shot into the drink. Insert annoyed mumble. I stomp over to the drop area and hit a fine shot, two putt for five.

Shit.

Eight over, fifteen down.

EIGHTEENTH HOLE:
Par 4, 398 yards

The finishing hole. I'm certain no other golfer in the history of this course has had a round quite like mine today. I'm at eight over, which is still on track for my best round ever and would put me at a nice, tidy eighty. A birdie would be nice of course. I've never shot below an eighty-five, so getting into the seventies would be groovy, man.

The hole is a semiblind tee shot. Meaning you can see everything you need to see from the tee but cannot see the green. A strong tee shot leaves you with a chance to go for the green in two but means carrying a pond that protects the front, and you can often have a slightly downhill lie for that shot. Always interesting hitting something around 160 yards, having to carry 140 of them, with the hill cheating you of loft.

Anyway, tee shot first, figure out the second shot when you get there. I'm in the middle of my backswing when I hear the unmistakable *Muuuuuuuhhhhh!*

The zombie slams into me, spilling me forward. I tumble over, losing the pistol from the small of my back as I recover. I still have the driver in my hand. We're facing each other, about five feet apart, but the zombie isn't attacking. He's just looking at me with his arms raised. I didn't hear him coming at all, nor do I know where he came from. That's pretty damn creepy. He's big, bigger than me, maybe six feet two inches and whatever big zombies weigh. He must have been a jock in his former life, though, at this point, the former jock only has one eye.

Muuuuuuuhhhhh! Louder this time. I can hear the echoes come back to us from the nearby ponds.

"Fuck you," I spit. "Fuck you, the horse you rode in on, and all the king's horses and all the king's men. You just made a big damn mistake, you lousy sonofabitch."

He's still not moving to attack, and I can't figure it out. Aside from the three back on the seventh hole chasing the squirrel, all I've ever seen them do is assault immediately and mindlessly. He's just there a few feet from me, looking at me, and I'm just about to turn and run back to the bag to get the shotgun when I see it. A flicker of his eye over my left shoulder, and I begin to rotate just in time for another zombie to crash heavily into my side, knocking the driver from my grip.

This collision really hurts. His shoulder drills me squarely in the ribs and snaps my neck sideways as we go down into a tangled tumble of limbs. He must have been running pretty fast when he hit me. How did I not hear that? That's gonna leave a helluva bruise. That is, if I survive this to be able to notice. As we stop rolling, I separate slightly from him and draw the KNIFE from its hilt on my left thigh. I've always loved the *shhhrrrring* sound a blade makes as it's withdrawn, but I take no enjoyment in it right now.

Wasting no time, I go after the newest zombie with twelve inches of gleaming, hardened steel and a shitty attitude. While he lurches for me with both arms, I duck under his grasping arms and into close range. Using the forward momentum, I slam the blade hilt-deep into his torso, just under his rib cage, and then rip sharply upward with all my strength. My arms are immediately covered with a spewing mess of zombie viscera. I can't get the KNIFE out—it must be hung up on a bone in there somewhere—so I let go of the handle as his body slackens and droops toward the ground. One of his hands drags loosely at my shirt and then falters away.

I know the other one has to be right on top of me, so I don't bother to look around. Instead, I dive off to the right for the driver and roll through to my knees. My side is an aching lump of agony—I bet he broke a rib or two—as I raise the club to a rough batting stance. Jock zombie is right there, closing in.

I swing the club, proper golf form be damned—sorry again, instructor people—and mash the oversized head into the side of his melon, which explodes as if Gallagher nailed it with his mallet. I hit him as he's falling. I hit him as he flops to rest on the side of the tee boxes, spraying blood in all directions. Several sprays hit my pants, but nothing falls on my skin. All the rage I've felt today from finding and losing the woman, all the anger and hurt from being left alone these past months, and probably some leftover teenage angst erupts into my assault. I'm not seeing clearly. I'm just hitting him over and over again. At some point, the club head flies off. Doesn't matter. I keep hitting him with the shaft. Then I start stabbing him with it a few times for good measure. After what seems like ages, I stop and look down at my handiwork.

That's one dead fuckin' zombie, pretty much zombie pudding at this point. I'm not proud, but I do feel better. I'm a smidge sad though. I really liked that club.

Flinging the now-useless shaft to the side, I pick up the pistol and replace it in my pants as I walk over to the first zombie. I put my foot on his neck—better safe than sorry, despite the gaping hole in his chest—and remove the KNIFE with both hands. It must have been caught on a rib or something because it takes a minute before popping free and slinging a wet trail of blood and guts across the cart path.

I go back to the bag and grab my 3-wood. I haven't used it today. It flies true and lands with a series of bounces well out in the fairway. Apparently, golf with zombies is good for my score overall.

I hike out to the ball, noticing I'm still on the flat—so, maybe driver isn't the right choice here—and about 170 yards out. A good 4-iron will get me there. From up here, you've got a panoramic view out over the sprawl of the course, the clubhouse, and the parking lot. I parked right up front under a tree and in a handicapped spot. What? Don't judge! No one's going to have a problem with it. They're all so handicapped they're dead.

Another good swing, and the ball lands on the back of the green and wanders left toward the pin. I'm going to have about fifteen feet between me and an eighty, without much trouble in between. As I cross the bridge over the pond, I think I see movement in the parking lot, but it could be anything—a critter, a zombie, a zombie critter, who knows—and is 100 yards away, so no worries.

I'm not kidding myself about birdie chances from here—it's a little downhill and a right-to-left break. The golf gods agree and leave the first putt four feet short. I walk over to drop the flagstick and line up carefully. Dead center of the cup, with a sweet rattle as the ball settles.

Eight over, sixteen down. An eighty. No one to watch, no one to tell. I feel pretty damn empty, but still pleased.

SHOTGUN FINISH

I put all the golf paraphernalia into the assorted pouches and pockets in my bag: tees, ball marker, ball mark repairer, and the ball. I shrug the bag onto my shoulders for the walk to the car and am relieved it's for the last time today. I ache, my muscles are tired, and I'm just emotionally spent.

As I crest the rise from the green up to the base of the clubhouse and cart-return area, I see what the movement was from a few minutes ago. There are at least twenty zombies standing near my car, and I'm sure it's not just to admire the shiny paint. I realize this must have been what I was seeing earlier in the round—the rotten bastards were *gathering* over here to get me. Unreal. Methinks they're smarter than I've previously given them credit for.

There are no alternatives. I don't feel like running; I'm too tired. I set the bag down to my side and sling the rifle over one shoulder, make sure the pistol is situated just right, and check on the KNIFE—much more fun when you say it that way, even in your head, and especially with an Australian accent— and pull the shotgun out of the bag, slipping the Darth Vader club head cover off of it. I haven't used that today either.

In golfing parlance, a shotgun start is when players go to every hole on the course and start to play at the same time. This is usually done during the cold weather months so eighteen groups can all finish a round at the same time, before it gets dark. Today, I'm going to have a shotgun finish. The odds don't look great from here, but I'm going to give it my best shot or two.

It's starting to rain, with a faint grunt of thunder rolling over the hills in the distance. "Hey!" I shout.

Heads swivel toward me, and I do one of those cool-guy, one-armed moves to chamber the first round in the shotgun.

"Bring it!"

Part Two: Five Play

CHAPTER 1

I'm covered in blood. I look like someone just dumped a barrel of viscera and blood over my head like a sick Gatorade bath. It's more their blood than mine, though. I'm still standing, so I think that means I won, but I would have preferred Gatorade for sure. After my ammo ran out, the last two had to go down the hard way—for all of us. The first one took the KNIFE—Australian accent reminder—through her throat and went down in a gargling heap. The second one I had to beat to death with the shotgun. Somewhere along the way, the stock broke free, so I guess I will have to find another one in the neighborhood. It's good to be the guy with the guns.

I stand in the parking lot, surveying the carnage of one man versus at least two dozen zombies or whatever they like to be called. Who knows? Before this giant mess, the only zombies were those in movies and on TV shows, but no one *really* knew what they were like. Before today, they seemed like a shuffling, mindless mob of unselective flesh-eating machines that were fairly easy to kill once you got the hang of it. It was rare to see groups of more than three or four together.

My lesson for the day—aside from a mental note to carry far more ammunition next time—is that they're both smarter and faster than I've seen before. Also, they seem to be gathering in larger groups. That can't be good.

I walk back down to my golf bag, taking stock of how I feel in addition to being a red-spattered mess of gore and whatever other mystery bits and pieces are stuck to me. My right shoulder is deeply sore, probably from a combination of the multiple recoils of the shotgun and when one of them grabbed and wrenched my arm during the close-in fighting. I think I've cracked a rib on the same side. I can feel fresh blood trickling down the side of my head from a cut just above my left ear. My fault, that one. I was using the KNIFE at the end and made the mistake of trying to stab zombie one, but the blade bounced off her skull and nicked me on the recoil. One of my knees feels a little squishy, too, like it's not tightly in place, but it doesn't feel alarming. None of my injuries seem significant individually, but after all the periodic combat through the golf round, the golf round itself, and the horrible disappointment with the woman preceding this melee, I'm exhausted. The adrenaline high is starting to dissipate, and I need to get home before I crash and the rest of them find me. I know I'm not so lucky as to have killed *all* of them.

I just drag the bag behind me as I return to the car, sliding the key fob out of one of the upper zippered pockets and unlocking it—old habits die harder than zombies. It's an effort, but I hoist the bag into the trunk and remove a couple of spare clips for the .45 handgun from a milk crate I keep in the car, along with water, shotgun shells, and granola bars for just in case. Sagging into the driver's seat, I fire up the car with a satisfying grunt and ease out of the lot, not bothering to avoid running over a couple of zombies on the way out. Just in case they weren't dead, dead. Aiming for the head is always a good idea whether with a Goodyear radial or a shotgun or a baseball bat.

***

I spend the next couple weeks recovering, resting, and thinking.

After the world went to shit, I had done an awful lot of just waiting around. Once I had been through all the houses in the neighborhood, run all my "shopping" trips to the local stores, and built my little fortress, my days were a lot emptier. Or less full, depending on what your psychologist tells you.

Over the past decade or so, we had been accustomed to the constant barrage of information and input via the internet and its assorted brethren—thank *you*, Al Gore. Then, it had all been silenced in a virtual heartbeat.

I had been a reluctant and limited consumer of the wave of mostly useless information. You couldn't entirely dodge the never-ending, breathless reports of celebrity and noncelebrity misdeeds, sports scores, and feats—horror stories of what supposedly next-door-normal people would do to other humans and the minutiae of the "all things are reported" new paradigm.

Now that the real horror story has arrived and the useless information is gone, I'm realizing how exhausting it all was.

The shame of it is, while I had avoided it like the plague, I still remember stuff about the Kardashians.

But the resting and thinking did me some good. It helped me realize I hadn't explored much outside of about a ten-square-mile area, and I'd had family in both Colorado and upstate New York before all this.

It's time to start thinking about traveling out there to try and find them or at least find out what may have happened to them. Winter's over, gasoline is cheaper than it has ever been, and I've got a badass truck to haul all my stuff. I'm going to start packing and preparing tomorrow … or at least soon.

CHAPTER 2

The next morning brought a blazing hot, middle-spring, Carolina kind of day. The humidity was high enough that when I sat on my front porch sipping coffee, my forehead was speckled with beads of sweat before I was halfway through the first cup. It just felt thick and heavy out, with the threat of all-day thunderstorms looming ominously off on the western horizon. Fat, wet clouds in every direction told me if I was going to pack, it had better be in the garage.

Weapons were the easy part of packing—just bring two of everything and a shitload of ammo. I even threw my katana sword in there. It's solid-feeling yet decorative. I'd come across it during one of my excursions throughout the neighborhood. I had been able to sharpen it to a wicked edge—I did have a *lot* of free time on my hands after all. It's unlikely to chop through a bamboo tree or anything, but against a semisquishy zombie critter, I liked my odds.

Some clothes, shoes, jackets, gloves, hats, and toiletries—all the things you'd bring on a normal camping trip. Plus a sleeping bag, a couple flashlights with extra batteries, matches and lighters for making a fire, and lots of food along with several pots, pans, and utensils.

Even though I'd been able to get gas from any gas station with a siphon pump I had rigged up, it made sense to throw a bunch of full gas cans into the back. It was easy enough to find multiple lawnmowers from nearby houses and consolidate into one another. I was surprised by the number of riding lawnmowers I came across since the lots in the neighborhood were no more than a quarter of an acre. Hello, lazy people. But, it was to my benefit since I now had roughly fifty extra gallons of fuel across several cans in the bed of the truck in case I got hung up at some point. It was a thirsty monster, maybe getting fifteen miles per gallon. I planned to be out there for a while, and who knew what I was going to find once I headed north.

At one point, I had tossed my wallet into the cab, so I head back into the house for some cash too. While I doubt anywhere else is much different from North Carolina, what if I get to like Maryland and it's normal and I have to pay for stuff? Strangely, that thought almost keeps me in place. I miss uninfected people and some parts of my old life, but I'm also oddly content with the new reality. No work, no noise, no rules, no waves of bullshit information about nothing. The zombies and I get along fine. I shoot, stab, or beat them to death, and they die. What's not to like? It all works for me.

That being said, I can decide on whether to go or not at any time, so I go back into the house and upstairs to one of the guest bedrooms. One of the closets is practically full of money. For whatever reason, I had initially collected a lot of cash as I went through all the houses over the winter, thinking in "old" terms that it would be helpful at some point. As it turns out, of course, everything is free now in my neck of the woods. But for some reason, I had never bothered to get rid of my stash. Now, I have a duffel bag full of mixed bills.

I can see it now—cruising through Pennsylvania at 100 miles per hour, getting pulled over and busted for being a gun-toting, money-laundering drug dealer. *Yes, officer, these guns and cash are all mine. You see, in North Carolina, we've been overrun by zombies, don't you know. I'm sure they'll be here soon, sir.*

The sun is shining sharply through the windows, lighting the dust motes sprinkled in the air—no changes in that little part of the world from then to now. As I step toward the closet, I see shadows flicker outside, like something had walked between the sun and the window. I don't react since something like that isn't really unusual, but then I remember the new reality I live in. People don't just walk by windows on a regular basis anymore.

What the hell was that?

"That" turned out to be a game changer.

I have a great view down the street from this window, and I just stare through the glass at the world's weirdest parade, ever. A shambling mob of zombies is making their way up the street to my house. They're in all shapes and sizes—though not too many chubby ones—with different degrees of zombieism, some male, some female, some hard to tell. I count somewhere north of fifty of them. But the most interesting by far are the two females at the head of the procession.

One is a zombie, that's obvious, though she looks somewhat "newer" than most of the zombies I've encountered. In relative terms, she's cleaner and less contaminated-looking. Her straggly, black hair drapes across her forehead and obscures her eyes, like a black curtain blocking out the sun.

The other female is a nonzombie. Her hands are being held firmly behind her back, and she's struggling like mad against her two male captors, with her chest thrust out and head whipping side to side in obvious panic. They close in on the foot of the driveway after a few moments, and I can hear the low rumble of an assembling crowd of humans settle to a stop. Well, one human anyway and a passel of something unholy, at least in my eyes. One might suspect God had different ideas lately.

Now what? Far too many critters for me to dispose of this time. I have plenty of guns, ranging between handguns and long guns, but I would never be able to kill all fifty before being overwhelmed, even if shooting from behind the stockade wall surrounding my property. It would just never work. Plus, there is the question of the seemingly uninfected woman at the front.

What's the story there?

I head downstairs, picking up a second .45 off the half wall at the top of the stairwell. I always, always carry one with me, along with several spare magazines, but multiplying my firepower seems prudent just in case. I walk down and through the ground floor of the house and step back out into the blazing sunlight. Darn, I forgot my sunglasses.

Keeping the gun in my left hand, I walk down the driveway to my makeshift gate and unlock it before swinging it open just enough for me to first peek and then slide through. Just like in the horror movies from the old days, I want to be ready to jam it shut right away if anything tries to sneak through. Considering the odds, and the number of zombies I'd just fought and barely killed a few weeks back, this is easily the dumbest thing I've ever done in my life since that one time in band camp. I mean, college.

Anyway, I wait because there is obviously a point to the parade, though I can't imagine why they haven't already fallen on the human woman and reduced her to a crimson smear on the street. Based on the look in the eyes of her restrainers, this isn't far from what they have in mind, but they are being held back somehow. Is this a trick to get me out in the open? Maybe she isn't really clean but rather a gussied-up, pretty zombie?

The female zombie steps forward, followed by the two monsters and their captive. When she sees me, the woman's eyes bug out even farther than they were, if that's possible. I notice then she has a makeshift gag in her mouth that encircles her head, making her cheeks bulge. As they pause at the base of my driveway, I step farther away from the gate and slip the second .45 out of the waistband of my shorts. I'm as ready as I can be for whatever they have in mind. If this goes south, it's going to be over quickly, but I'm going to take a crapload of them with me if I can't get through the gate in time.

With a subtle gesture of her fingers, the zombie leader ushers the pair of handlers forward to stand parallel with her. They continue to hold their captive at arm's length and clearly are handing her over to me. *What the fuck is this all about?*

We stand roughly twenty feet apart, and then the zombie gal moves a few steps toward me. I'm able to get a good look at her as she moves forward. Before all this, she must have been attractive; she has a well-proportioned figure and moves easily as opposed to the occasionally stuttering movements of her peers. Again, I'm struck with the thought that she must be somehow newer than the others. As she moves to within ten feet and comes to a stop, she sweeps her hair away from her face and fixes me with a glare from two stunning, pale blue—but bloodshot—eyes burning out from what had clearly once been a lovely face. I think I recognize her as someone from the neighborhood, but I'm not certain since the changes wrought by zombiehood seem to vary across the breed.

Another gesture and the trailing trio approaches, the woman still struggling, and I raise one of the pistols unconsciously toward the one holding her on the left. At that, the mob grunts and takes a collective step forward but stops when the gal zombie shakes her head slightly. As the pair of big fellas draw to a stop, they push the woman forward. She pauses about halfway between them and me, and then clearly decides that the guy with the guns and lack of apparent hunger for human flesh is the right team to be on. She steps just past me and begins to work on removing the gag now that her arms are free.

I look at the leader. Her face is impassive, as if she has all the time in world. I wonder again what this is all about. I know the woman doesn't have a clue, so I try something.

"What is this?"

A shrug and then a gesture with both hands in obvious mimicry of, *We're giving her to you.*

"Why?" I'm sure it's not because they are giving me a prize for being the alpha male in the 'hood.

What comes next makes me want to throw up. By now, my new friend is loose from the gag and is standing closer to me, though not too close, like she is going to wait to pass judgment on me too.

The zombie queen cradles her arms and rocks them in an obscene mockery of a person rocking a baby. The woman gasps beside me.

"Baby? What does a baby have to do with anything?" I'm lost here.

Another immediately understandable gesture. She brings pinched fingers from a cupped hand to her mouth. *Food.*

My stomach somersaults at the idea.

"You want us to make babies, so you can have something to eat ... " I pause, seeing what's in it for us too. "And you'll leave us alone if we create a food supply for you."

A nod. Unreal. We're communicating perfectly. I should have had so much luck with women in the past.

"What's to stop me from blowing your head clean off?" I ask as I calmly level the pistol in my right hand at her left eye. "You're the leader of this fucked-up clan, and maybe they'll all run away if you're a dead bag of bones."

With this, the crowd bares their teeth and moves two rapid steps forward but halts abruptly. I hear nothing, but it is unmistakable that they've stopped because they've been "told" to stop, not because one guy with a gun is going to win a conflict.

Zombie ESP? C'mon.

Her eyes never leave my face, and her expression never changes. She shrugs again and turns partly toward the rest of her crew, another clear signal. *You kill me. They kill you. Get it?*

A dilemma. I'm going to take the human woman into the house for sure; that's the easiest decision of the day. Company, someone to talk to, finally. But, getting this person pregnant? Creating food for the army of the dead? And we can only have one baby at a time after nine months, following whatever form courtship takes in the new world. That's not enough to do anything for their collective hunger. Something else must be afoot, though that's going to have to roll around in my head for a good long time.

One last question. "How will you know she's going to have a baby and that we're not just faking it?"

Another shrug and then one more gesture. She leans toward the woman and takes an exaggerated intake of breath through her nose. Jesus.

"You can smell it?"

A final nod.

"Okay. She comes in with me, you leave us alone, and we make babies. Deal." I wave my hand dismissively behind my back to show the new woman this is not a serious statement and to reassure her she hasn't just gone from the frying pan into the bonfire.

The queen fixes me with her scathing, bloodshot eyes for a long moment and then slowly turns away and steps through her followers, who part to let her through, and begins to walk back down the gently sloping street. I have a final thought.

"Wait!" I shout. All of them turn toward me. "Can you talk?"

Her baleful gaze holds me for a few seconds, and from where I stand, I can't tell if the gleam in the corners of her eyes is anything other than the angle of the sun. It might be a last vestige of humanity. For once, she makes no "reply," just turns back around and goes on her way, trailing her bedraggled procession behind her.

Holy shit. None of this is on the to-do list for today or makes a pile of sense, but what really does anymore?

I turn to the woman, try an encouraging smile, and gesture toward the open gate. She shrugs—which pretty much sums up my communication with women for the day—and then she leads the way in. I shove the gate shut with a satisfying clunk as the catch engages, then I replace the brace back across the doors and into its brackets. We begin walking up the driveway, separated by a few feet, but in the world after the apocalypse, we're together courtesy of the queen of the zombies.

And then there were two.

CHAPTER 3

You have to find out; you have to be sure. You know this.
Yes, I do, and I already regret what's going to come next since this will be a super way to get off on the right foot with my new roommate.

We make it to the front door, which is still hanging open, and I gesture for her to go in first. She nods hesitantly and then walks inside, stopping in the foyer and turning to face me as I swing the door closed behind us.

"Strip," I say. "Please."

She looks sharply up at me, gently shaking her head as if she hadn't heard me clearly. "Excuse me?"

"I'm sorry, but this is nonnegotiable." I keep my face closed and my pistol in my hand.

"Are you *kidding*?" she shouts. "You think you're going to get me to take my clothes off, right here in the middle of the goddamn front hallway five seconds after we've met? Are you going to rape me? You're in for a big, goddamn surprise if you think that's what's happening." I think I made her mad.

"I'm sorry, but I have to check you." I pause before continuing in as calm a voice as I can muster. "I need to make sure you're not bitten, not infected, not some kind of trick by that smart zombie. I know this is putting us off on the wrong foot, but I'm going to be safe and selfish." I hate this, but there's no two ways about it under the new rules. Some manners have to wait, and we're going to get introduced in a ridiculous way because I don't want to know her name before seeing her naked, checking for bites, and blowing her head off if she actually has been bitten.

How's that? At least in the old days, you'd know someone's name before seeing them naked. Well, most of the time, I suppose.

Tears well in her eyes, likely from both anger and fear, as she stares at me. "And if I don't?"

There's a challenge in her voice that I like. This isn't a weak person. She survived everything over the winter months, only to be faced with her first human in a while, one who is nicely holding a pistol and telling her to take her clothes off before proper introductions.

"You go back to them," I say with a shrug. "I can guess, and so can you, what they'd do if you showed up back outside. They'd think you've either been rejected by me and won't make babies for zombie food or something else. Either way, I think taking your clothes off inside a house with another human is the lesser of two evils, but it's your call." I've been accused of being too logical in the past, but it would be hard to find fault with me on this one.

She starts to say something and then stops herself. Instead, she raises a dirty hand to wipe away the tears now flowing from the corner of her left eye. It leaves a smudge across her face from eye to ear, almost like an '80s new wave band's makeup.

"You're not expecting to make babies for that … that … *thing*, are you?" That comes out in a smaller voice. I'm much bigger than she is and I have the gun, so I can see why her fear is beginning to outweigh the anger and indignation.

"We'll worry about that way, *way* down the road." I smile cautiously, feeling stupid for doing so, but I want to reassure her on that one point anyway. "But right now we have to get past this. I've got to be sure you're not twelve hours from being some kind of zombie Trojan Horse sent in to get me. I've killed a crapload of them, and they can't be happy about that. You need to not be one of them." I shrug and repeat, "I'm sorry." And then I just wait. Silence is one of the most amazing tools in the world, and I'm going to find out if it still works now.

She stares back at me with a firm set to her jaw. She looks at the door, then at me, and then to the floor. A sigh. She raises her eyes back to me, staring directly at me. The tears start again as she reaches across her torso for the bottom of her shirt and then stops.

"I'm not wearing a bra." She looks mortified as she mumbles this.

"Then I guess you'll be naked faster and this will be over sooner, won't it?" I say, wondering which conversation is less sane: this one or the one I had with the zombie queen.

"Oh. All the way naked." Not a question, not a statement, but a little of both. I just nod.

My mind flickers back to the one time in college when my buddies and I had managed to cajole, beg, negotiate, and perhaps grovel with some of our female friends to play strip poker. It was first semester freshman year, and we had been working for weeks—like any self-respecting idiots who now live on their own for the first time—on getting them to give in and play. We were sure we were going to win something. We were thrilled when they finally said yes, particularly since one of the girls was wearing a one-piece, sweater-dress thingy. That meant we were literally one hand from seeing bra and underpants. In those pre-internet days, seeing bra and underpants was worth fantasizing about since the closest you could usually get was either scoring an adult magazine or looking in the right section of the Sears catalog—of course, I ended up not seeing a damn thing, no matter how closely my friends told me to inspect each and every picture. As our luck would have it, the girls lost exactly zero hands, and my buddy was completely nude after five.

But I digress. That did, however, suck all the fun out of it. Carrying on …

"My name is Eve."

Shit. Now I know her name. She'd better be clean.

"Okay, Eve." I nod loosely, indicating for her to resume disrobing.

With that, she shrugs her filthy, blue shirt over her head, revealing pale white shoulders, breasts, and stomach. It's cooler in the house with a light breeze coming through the open windows, and I can't help but notice her nipples tightening as it cascades across her. With some effort, I pull my eyes back up to hers. It's been a long while.

She kicks her sneakers off to the side and then shimmies out of her pants next, leaving a pair of grubby, mismatched socks and, of all things, a red thong.

A thong. In frickin' zombie world.

Eve stops and looks at me. I admit, I'm curious to ask why on earth she is wearing a thong, but I decide to save that one for later.

I simply nod again, telling her she needs to continue. Another sigh. She reaches down for the socks and slips them off first. Then she closes her eyes and drops her drawers—what there is of them.

I look at her, trying to keep this clinical. She's thin—which isn't surprising given what's left for food supplies—maybe thirty-five or so. She has brown hair that brushes her shoulders and is tangled in a wild nest. She's slender in the chest, not needing a bra but not totally flat-chested either. I try to avoid looking at the tuft of hair between her legs, but I'm a man who hasn't had any kind of female company in half a year. She's attractive in a regular kind of way. She has a nice figure and delicate, feminine features. So shoot me for having functioning eyes.

I walk around her slowly, scanning her from head to toe from each side, seeing nothing. I tell her to lift her feet up one at a time, which she does with a slight totter.

Nothing.

"Okay. You can get dressed now." I turn my back for some reason. I can hear the sounds of her getting dressed, and then she walks around in front of me and moves up pretty close.

"Bastard. I hope you enjoyed the show." And with that, she marches off toward the back of the house, spine straight, angry body language virtually pouring out of her.

Eve. Clean Eve.

CHAPTER 4

It's a good thing I've had some practice over the preceding months with peace and quiet. The silence in the house over the next few hours is thunderous. I can't really blame her—she's had a big day. In a way, I'm glad for silence since this has been so sudden. I have to admit, I've gotten comfortable being alone. It's going to be weird having to adapt to another person in the house, especially since I have to make sure I don't shoot her if she gets up to pee in the middle of the night.

I busy myself with the usual: checking my weapons to be sure they're clean, arranging food supplies—and being suddenly aware they're going to diminish twice as quickly now—checking on the water collection, and then wondering what this means for my planned trip out of hell into, well, probably more hell.

I'm lying on the couch, reading a farming book as the late afternoon shadows start to lengthen across the living room. I'm in that vague state between awake and nodding off in the warmth, reading sentences about seed placement and moisture requirements over and over, when Eve walks into the room. I sit up, trying to shake the fog away quickly.

"Can I have something to eat and drink? I've had nothing for a few days."

Her face is tear-streaked, more so than when she had stomped out of the room earlier, and her eyes are puffy. Yup, big day.

"Sure. There's food over in the kitchen pantry. I hope you like canned stuff since that's about it at this point. I can heat it up on the grill for you. Water is in the bedroom down the hall to the left. Help yourself."

Eve walks to the pantry first, glances up and down at its contents, and then goes onward to the water room. Really, it's the water room. Floor to ceiling cases of bottled water. One of the biggest surprises for me is how much water I go through each day for routine things: brushing my teeth, cleaning in the kitchen, and more. Now, I have to source everything from bottles, and I go through them like mad. For once, I'm pleased with the American obsession with bottled water that was more expensive than gasoline, which is saying something.

When she returns, she has one empty bottle in hand and is halfway through a second. Turning back to the pantry, she shifts her weight to one hip, browses the menu, and chooses a can of vegetable soup. Then, she replaces it and grabs a can with chicken as well as vegetables. Soup isn't the sexiest meal in the world, but at least for getting veggies and meat all in one place, it's now maybe the best thing going.

Without making eye contact, she starts banging her way through drawers and cabinets looking for a can opener and pot—this bothers me a little bit since I'm not used to the regular noise of the world. I get off the couch, go into the kitchen, and get them out. I open the can and pour the soup into the pot, then I walk outside to start the grill.

One of my grills has a side burner, which is super and what I use the most since fresh meat is long gone, and I'm not quite ready for hunting, prepping, and so on—that book lurks on the built-in shelves next to the massive, dormant flat-screen TV.

I cook the soup to a nice bubbling simmer and then bring it in, find a bowl, and pour it for her without a word. She glances at me but says nothing. She then utterly destroys the soup in only a couple minutes with groans of pleasure along the way. Guess she isn't kidding about not eating for a few days; I know how that goes and it's miserable.

To think, I used to be "starving" if a meeting got scheduled during lunch. I'd be pissy and my stomach would be growling. I wouldn't focus on the meeting but rather on the clock and the indignity of being forced to wait for food. For the first few days after everything happened and I was in hiding, I'd eaten odds and ends of snacks from my own pantry. I was too good to eat the canned food cold at first and of course, was not going to start a grill to draw attention from the hordes of zombies infesting the area. That changed after less than twenty-four hours. I laugh now when I think back to the guy who took his first bite of cold ravioli and grimaced like he'd been forced to eat dog shit. How things change.

"Do you have anything stronger?" Her first words in a few minutes and with less of an edge than when she'd asked for food and water.

"Stronger than soup?"

She grins a little. "Stronger than water."

"Yeah. I've got a rather well-stocked liquor cabinet there in the butler's pantry. I'm a little light on mixers, and the ice machine is on the fritz, but take whatever you want." Another small smile from her, and I start to think this is going to be okay.

She rattles around the booze and settles on a bottle of Jack Daniel's whiskey. Surprisingly, she skips a glass and takes a long pull directly from the bottle. She coughs as the burn reaches her throat and stomach, then she wipes her mouth on her sleeve.

"Thanks. I needed that." She grins a little again. "I haven't had a drink in who knows how long, and God knows, with all that's happened, I've wanted one. Or two. Or ten."

"You're welcome. Please, make yourself at home, such as it is. There's lots of food, bedrooms are on the second floor, and the toilet is a fresh-air model out back toward the golf course." I'm watching her closely as she seems to be winding down after a long, second swig of the Captain. I can see the tension release from her face and body.

She looks at me for a long moment, takes a third draft of the whiskey, and then sets the bottle down on the granite counter with a *thunk*.

"God, that stuff's rough straight, isn't it? I used to drink it back in school, but only with Coke, and it was mostly Coke since I'd get bombed too quickly, and then the night would turn into one of those college stories you'd kinda regret later." A wistful smile as she hearkens back to maybe happier—or, at least, less zombie-infested—memories. "Mmm. More water would be good."

Eve walks back to the water room, and I notice she's not walking nearly as straight as she had the last time. My guess is she's significantly dehydrated, definitely undernourished, and exhausted. I don't sleep well anymore, even inside my little fortress, and I'm willing to bet she's in the same, if not worse, boat.

By the time she makes it back into the room, she's finished more than half of another bottle of water and manages to bounce off the wall just a smidge as she enters the kitchen. Clearly the bottle of Jack is working its magic on top of everything else, which is probably a good thing.

"What's your name?" she asks.

I tell her and she nods.

"Did we know each other? I mean, before?" I shake my head no; I don't recognize her from the neighborhood.

There are a thousand houses in here, so there are "new" people you've never seen before, not to mention the normal turnover as people moved. I haven't kept to myself exactly, but I have been one of the few single people in the neighborhood. Most of the people I have met are guys on the golf course and my immediate neighbors.

Setting the bottle down too firmly on the counter so a miniature geyser shoots from the top, Eve says, "I'm beat, I'm a little drunk, I'm surrounded by a spiky fence, and I'm in a house with a guy I've just met who talks to zombies. I need to sleep. Please?"

I nod and walk her upstairs to show her the other bedrooms. When she decides on a room, I hand her some light blankets and sheets and close the blinds against the setting sun. She doesn't bother with much decorum. She throws the fitted sheet on the bed, kicks her shoes back off, drops onto the mattress like a stone, and then pulls the regular sheet over her. I draw the blanket up and then start walking out of the room.

"Hey," she says softly as I grab the doorknob, getting ready to close the door. "Thank you."

"Sleep well. You're as safe as you're going to be here, so try and get some rest." I turn to leave and hear her mumble something so I ask her to repeat.

"I can't have children," she says, her voice fading as she seems to sink deeper into the bed.

"Good night, Eve."

She sleeps for more than twenty-four hours.

CHAPTER 5

I'm an early riser. Now even more than in the past. Weekends, to me, were for doing as much as you possibly could, not for sleeping the free days away.

I have no idea what day it is anymore, mostly because it doesn't matter and partly because I don't want to bother keeping track of time. What's the point in spending any mental energy doing so? It's a day ending in "day," and they are mostly the same—stay out of trouble if you can.

Today is no different except now I have a roommate and a pseudo-deadline—*Oh, haha, I see what you did there!*— to consider. I sit on the back porch, looking out over the golf course, watching the dew sparkle in the very, very early sunlight and wondering what's next. All the house windows are open—they always are or it gets stuffy and I feel claustrophobic—so I hear Eve shuffling about in the kitchen. Probably looking for coffee, which I kind of have. Instant coffee brewed on the side burner of the grill in a tea pot. It beats the shit out of no coffee but not by much.

She comes out, blinking in the sharp sunlight reflected off the ponds that meander through the grounds of the neighborhood and golf course. Tired, obviously, though she just crashed as hard as I've ever seen someone. Well, a postcollege someone, at least. Her brown hair is even more askew than it was when she was delivered, and there is a spiderweb of sleep lines all over her face and neck.

I know that if I sleep longer than normal, I wake up disoriented, crabby, and generally out of sorts, so I walk past her without a word and find a second mug and come back out and hand it to her. "Coffee's over there on the grill. Like Fords in the old days—any way you like as long as it's black. But it's hot."

She nods and goes over to pour a cup and then stands there for a moment, glancing at the seating choices, clearly uncertain about something. There is a recliner over in the corner and a regular wooden chair next to the table where I'm sitting. I see; she's choosing between close and far. I get it—she doesn't want to be stupid and sit close to the maybe-dangerous stranger she's been commanded to sleep with or be rude to the maybe-dangerous stranger who is now providing some measure of sanctuary. The rules around all of that are brand new, whatever they are.

"I'm not going to bite you, Eve," I say with a wry smile as I catch the double meaning. "Sit wherever you want, have some coffee, and wake up. I have more food, too, when you're ready. We can talk whenever."

She nods again and sits near me, sipping slowly and looking out across the pretty, green vista stretching out below the patio. In any other time, this would be about as good as it gets. But, I'm not used to company, she's not used to not being chased by monsters, and there is an elephant in the room.

You're not in a room. Can you say it like that when sitting outside? Just asking for a friend.

As if reading my mind, she finally speaks. "What about the other thing?"

"You've got nothing to worry about there either. I know we just met, but I'm an old-fashioned kind of guy, even now when everything's crazy. So, that means we figure out how to live together and be friends if we can and take everything one day at a time. More than anything else, I want to figure out how to kill that bitch and her mob. That's it. You're welcome here, and I'm glad for your company. Good?"

One more nod, which is answer enough, I guess. She's quiet for a few more minutes as she finishes her coffee, eyes scanning the world. I watch her out of the corner of my eye. She looks at peace, despite the last couple days and months, which is a good thing.

We spend the next handful-plus days getting to know one another, getting used to having company and having to cohabitate after months alone for both of us. She's a Charlotte-area native as it turns out—one of the few—and is younger than I'd thought at thirty-one. Once she cleans all the dirt and grime off, she's even prettier, in a normal girl kind of way versus an eye-catching, across the room, "whoa-look-at-the-supermodel" kind of way. She'd taken a bath in the pond that lines the fourteenth and seventeenth holes. I'd stood guard with my back turned and shotgun at the ready.

Eve tells me her backstory. She's newly divorced—before the zombies, when pretty much everyone got divorced—from a husband who she assumes is gone like everyone else. He'd traveled in a sales role for a local NASCAR race team; she'd stayed home working on a novel and doing some freelance magazine writing to keep her skills sharp and some money flowing in. Their relationship had faltered as soon as they'd found out they were unable to have children; somewhat predictably, he'd started working longer hours, traveling more, and talking less. They separated somewhat amicably and sadly about a year before the apocalypse. Sadness touches her eyes as she tells me about all this, though from her words, it's hard to tell which part of it she's sad about.

She's also an amateur golfer of some accomplishment, playing in college and in regional tournaments. That solves one thing—we're *not* going to play golf together. I don't feel any urge to get out on the course again anytime soon. I decide not to tell her about my most recent round; no need for her to hear about what happened to the last woman I'd met.

What strikes me more than anything else as I get to know her is that she's, indeed, peaceful by nature. We don't hang out together all the time. Sometimes we're in the same room and we talk; sometimes we're not. But I walk into rooms fairly frequently to find her gazing out a window, looking relaxed and composed. I'm not wound particularly tight either, other than constantly keeping my eyes open for danger, but there is a stoic calm she exudes; I feel more settled when I'm around her. I think she's carrying some mental baggage as a result of the failed marriage and maybe whatever else we all drag around with us from life, but she is easy to be around and is a kind person. I count myself lucky that they brought someone nice. On that note, the zombies have remained true to the queen's word. During those two weeks, we never see one come any closer than a few hundred yards away, and none of them ever begin to approach us. That doesn't mean I'm going to walk around unarmed—I'm going to take any chance I get to whittle their population down, but with none of them coming close, I have no reason to expend ammo.

I mean, I don't know pregnancy, but I do recall something about eleven weeks being when a woman can safely share she's expecting. I guess that is when the zombies will be able to smell a baby. Eve just arrived two weeks ago. So, by my calculations we have about ... nine weeks? ... to do *something*. Whether it is leave, try to kill all the zombies, or something else.

***

One night, I'm lying awake in bed, just listening to the sounds of the night as the breeze carries warm, spring air across me. I'm glad the inevitable nighttime screams of the first days of the new world are long gone.

Those nights had been horrible; hiding wherever I could, feeling exhausted and scared to death that one of them would find me. The thirst. The hunger. The shrill screaming from other humans being caught echoed across the ponds throughout the neighborhood, making anything more than fitful, fearful sleep impossible.

Mother Nature has begun to reclaim the world and maybe scrub it clean since then. I hear the whirring of a variety of insects. There are some light crashes in the natural area behind the house, which probably means squirrels or possums or whatever are out and about.

Then, I hear a noise in the house. I'm immediately 100 percent awake and attuned to the sounds of the night, both inside and outside the house. Reaching for the gun on the bedside table, I start to get out of bed when Eve walks into the room. I stop and look at her silhouette in the doorway. The ghostly light from the moon through the window puts enough illumination on her for me to see she's only wearing a baggy T-shirt and is bare-legged.

"Are you okay?" I ask, placing the gun back down.

Without a word, she walks to the other side of the king-size bed, slips under the covers, and scoots over so her back is pressing against me, but she's facing away. I can feel the heat and softness of her body against mine. Luckily, I still wear boxers to bed out of old habit.

"Now I am," she whispers.

I lie on my back with a woman snuggled against me in the empty world and listen to her breathing settle and smooth out. I think about it all, wondering where this is going to go and what I should do. I feel her warmth, and it strikes me that it has been almost half a year since I've even touched another person. It's good. I sleep like a teenager, warm and heavy.

The next few days and nights are similar. We get to know one another, and we scour neighborhoods farther away from home for weapons, tools, food, and water. Some nights, she comes into my room to sleep next to me; some nights she doesn't. It's a comfortable routine.

But the clock's ticking.

CHAPTER 6

Routine, schmoutine. It all changes again one morning. I'm slowly surfacing from the depths of sleep in the too-warm room and bed when I hear noises outside and know they're back. Glancing over, I can see Eve is gone. She either left during the night or was already awake. I then hear some shouting and cursing through the window. That's new.

I get dressed quickly and hurry downstairs. I find her leaning against one of the windows at the front of the house that has a clear view over the fence and down the street. She's holding a mug of coffee in both hands and against her pink lips. The steam from the mug drifts upward to touch her nose before dissipating. I watch her in silence for a moment, looking at her profile.

She senses me and turns slightly as I come into the room. Picking up a second mug, she hands it to me and says, "You're going to need this. Look at that."

I look out the window to see the parade of madness is back. The zombie queen is out front, flanked by her two monstrous wingmen who hold a struggling woman. They're trailed by the horde of forty to fifty additional abominations shuffling their way up the street. The woman is a howling banshee, screaming at the top of her lungs in an incredible litany of swearing and fighting every single step as they drag her.

"I know how she feels," says Eve. "I thought they were taking me to some kind of ceremony where they were going to eat me slowly or convert me or something. Turned out it was a ceremony but not what I had been afraid of. We should go out there."

I agree and grab the two handguns, hand a shotgun to Eve, and we go outside to meet the group.

CHAPTER 7

The banshee has an astonishing vocabulary. She's throwing insults at her handlers, the queen, and apparently everyone who has ever done her wrong. The vitriol that spews from her mouth is an amazing blend of the timeless classics and some new things involving impossible physical contortions I've never heard. Safe to say, she's pissed. She also has an impressive imagination.

Her cursing stops when Eve and I walk through the gate and face the huge group. Her eyes go wide to see normal people, and she stops midcurse along the lines of what the zombies could do with their mothers' dogs.

The zombies, for their part, seem completely unfazed by the incredible display of profanity and anger coming from their prisoner. The behemoths are directed to give her to us. She goes to Eve immediately, and they stand together slightly behind me.

I face off again with the queen. We go through the same pantomime routine we did with Eve. Babies, food, and more. The new woman watches this with wild eyes, flipping back and forth between looking at me and the zombie engaged in our mockery of a conversation. We end at agreeing like before, but I have another question. Though I'm not sure how she's going to answer unless she really can speak.

"Even if we made two babies, that's not enough to feed all of you. So why?" I ask.

She waits for a moment and then pats her chest.

"They're for you?" She nods. "Still, that's not enough for you to survive on, especially if you have to wait nine months. So, what's the deal?"

At this, she waves her hand over her face in a circle. Her not-as-disgusting-or-deteriorated-as-the-others face. I ponder over this for a few moments, and then my stomach turns as I finally understand. Eve gasps, too, as she figures it out.

"You think it will keep you looking more human if you eat babies." I spit the words out in disgust. A zombie with vanity? A fountain of youth? I picture this aberration eating an infant and feel my hand tightening on the trigger of my gun. I want to shoot her so badly it's everything I can do to not pull the trigger. But I know we have nowhere near enough bullets to kill them all before we're overcome. So, I get ahold of myself, lower the gun, and vow then and there I'm going to kill this bitch someday, and slowly if possible.

"Get lost, you horror show." I feel tears in the corners of my eyes. This is just horrible.

Rather than retreat down the road like last time, she walks toward and then past me.

Closing in on Eve, she leans forward and takes a deep breath in through her nose. A pause. Then she bares her teeth, staring between the two of us, eyes blazing in anger. Her message is clear. *I know she's not pregnant.*

"Fuck you. Get lost." I have nothing witty.

They finally leave—one stumps along on an incomplete foot—taking a few minutes to disappear out of sight around the corner.

CHAPTER 8

The three of us watch the zombie mob until it moves out of sight. Then we go through the gate, up the driveway, and to the front door. Following the same routine as with Eve, we get indoors, and I turn to the new woman. She's much different than Eve—taller, thinner, and with a tan that says she's either been to tanning salons a lot in the past, or she's spent some time outside without sunscreen. She's attractive in a rough kind of way, with a mildly masculine-shaped face, strong cheekbones, blue eyes, and blond hair that's dark at the roots. This looks like a woman you wouldn't talk to in a bar until you've had a few, and then you would be surprised by the transformation in the morning. That being said, she would have been one of the first people you'd notice in said bar since men are preprogrammed to notice blondes and boobs, especially if they're combined into one package. Her face is so weathered, I take her for middle forties. Which means I've been given yet another woman who cannot have babies. The queen needs to do her homework better in the future, or we're never going to get along.

I can tell the new woman is bursting with questions, though she'd clearly followed the gist of the one-sided conversation. I couldn't anticipate what those questions would turn out to be, however.

"Strip," I say. "Please."

"What, you're gonna fuck me before we're even introduced? Is she gonna watch, or is she going to join in and we go three-way?" she asks as she tosses her head at Eve, who has an incredulous expression on her face. "Well, all right," she continues, without waiting for an answer. "I have to tell ya, it's been a bunch of months since I had a dick in me, and rubbin' a few out every week just hasn't been the same for me. Go ahead, do whatcha gotta do. Get that dick out and ready to go while I get naked."

I'm as speechless as I have ever been in my life. Glancing over at Eve, I see she's just as thunderstruck. I have never, *ever* heard a woman speak like this. Nor had I even imagined it in my most random, confused teenage fantasies.

After kicking her socks and shoes off, she stops for a second as she's grasping the bottom of her shirt across her midsection. "I gotta tell you ahead of time, I ain't wearing a bra on account of these amazing fake titties I got a while ago. Don't need one no more, though the perky nipples can be a bit pesky sometimes. Oh, and I might still have some crotch critters around. Had 'em a while back and think they've gone, but you never know."

Seriously? Did I miss the memo? In case of a zombie apocalypse, women shall no longer wear bras? This couldn't have come out beforehand?

I have to stop her before my head explodes. "No, please don't get the wrong idea. We need you to strip to make sure you haven't been bitten, so you don't turn into one of them and attack us in a few hours." I try to still my spinning head—she's unbelievable.

I see her face actually *fall* a little as she hears this. I think she's disappointed that we aren't going to have sex. *Good lord.*

"Oh. Okay, guess that makes some sense," she replies. With that, she shrugs her shirt over her head, revealing (as advertised) a pair of rather amazing boobs and perky nipples. *Cheers to her surgeon,* I think and then pull my eyes away from her chest. I try to remain impassive as she continues to undress. Of course, she isn't wearing underwear, which at least breaks one part of the tradition of stripping girls. I resolve then that any future women who are delivered will be checked by the other women, and I will take a pass. This is a bit much, and given how things have progressed from Eve to this one, we're likely to get Miley Cyrus next, God help us.

"Are you sure you don't want to all get naked? It's really been a while, and I've been bored. I could try a girl out." Both Eve and I shake our heads at the same time, likely both wondering what on earth just happened this morning and how it's going to change things.

"Okay then. Well, my name is Diane and ah'm sure glad to meet you. You can call me DeeDee. Everyone does." I'm certain she said DeeDee, not DD, but I'm not touching that one—just too easy. Besides, her boobs aren't *that* big.

We check her body carefully for bites. There are none, so we introduce ourselves, and I tell her to get dressed.

Three, three. I see, I see.

CHAPTER 9

We all go farther into the house and through somewhat of the same things I did with Eve when she arrived. DeeDee is starving. Besides talking like a trucker, she eats like one too, devouring three cans of soup—who knows where she puts it since she's as skinny as a rail. Although, she surprisingly skips the booze.

The girls chat in that incredible way women do when meeting someone new and finding what sounds like dozens of things to discuss. I listen vaguely and think.

I'm worried about change. It was quiet for months when it was just me and the Zs, and I've had a lot more time in my own head than is probably healthy by historic terms. As if on cue, DeeDee suddenly laughs a stunning, explosive cackle that must have echoed across countless barrooms in the past and shaken glasses on the shelves. I realize it has been forever since I've heard such a happy sound or any happy sound for that matter. I have to admit, despite the change in noise, I probably need both these women here. Not for procreation mind you, though that thought is lurking in the back of my mind too.

Do we have a responsibility to repopulate the world? Are humans deserving of continuing on? Eve says she can't have children. DeeDee has her crotch critters to consider and seems to be either too old or old enough where it would be risky for her to be pregnant. If we're supposed to fill the world with my children, this is an awfully inauspicious start.

I push those thoughts to the side and focus more on our immediate problem. There are roughly three weeks in the books since Eve's arrival, and she isn't pregnant nor will she be able to be so, apparently.

Nor are you banging her, so it's all a moot point isn't it? Ah, the peanut gallery. Didn't miss you.

Since clearly the zombie queen doesn't know or care about Eve's inability to get pregnant or otherwise, we have about eight weeks maybe before all hell breaks loose, and we have a massive conflict on our hands. Even with three of us, we can't kill all the zombies with firearms. The two women weigh likely a combined 210 pounds—hardly setting us up for success if we have to get up close and messy. We need something more efficient at killing them—a way to kill a bunch of them at once.

"Hey," says DeeDee. "Where am I gonna sleep? I'm fuckin' beat and could use a nap."

Just like Eve. Delivery, food and water, nap time.

"Those moaning, stumbling fuckers had been chasing me for four days before they finally caught me this morning," she continues before pausing for another deep gulp of water. "I just ran out of gas and lay down to rest for a few minutes inside a car in one of those houses down the road. Next thing I know, I dozed off and then one of those giant bastards was yanking me out by my hair. I thought I was a goner for sure, but he dragged me over to that kinda pretty zombie, and then they marched my ass up here and gave me to y'all."

Something she says strikes me—she was chased for four days. Eve had mentioned she had not eaten for several days when she came.

"Eve, were you chased too?" I ask, turning toward her.

"Yes. They flushed me from the house I'd been in for a while, and I was running ahead of them and hiding and moving from house to house for a few days. They caught me the same kind of way as DeeDee. When I finally couldn't run any longer and had to rest, they found me and brought me here to you. Why?"

"So, they just kept chasing you. Were you hiding each time?" I'm getting a thought here, and it's a very unsettling one—not like any of the other ones I've been having lately where they're all roses and chocolate.

"Yeah. I was hiding in attics, closets, storage areas, crawl spaces. They were definitely hunting for me. For the last house, I was in the powder room in the master bath, which was a mistake since the window didn't open. I had nothing to break it with, so I was cornered when they finished searching the house. I could hear them open and close doors, and from what it sounded like, they were going room to room." She stops, clearly remembering that morning from a few weeks back.

Shit. Systematic searches, for days.

First, there had been the two of them that had tried to trick me on the eighteenth tee. Then, there was the gathering in the parking lot at the end of my round of golf, as if they'd known or figured I was going to end up there. Then, this grouping around the zombie queen—who is clearly the leader and in careful control of the rest of the mob, not to mention her control was exerted without words.

Now, this revelation that they are smart enough to perform a thorough search of houses over the period of multiple days. And instead of eating the women as they catch them, they bring them to their leader and then to me.

Zombies are bad enough to begin with; now, I have to consider they're far more intelligent than I had originally expected and experienced. Plus, any group with a leader is more formidable than a loose collection. She is the key, but from what I've seen, she's also never alone. So, even if I can kill her, we'll be overrun by the rest of them.

We point DeeDee to one of the other upstairs bedrooms, which had been a boy's room before the world was flushed down the toilet. There's a nifty bunk bed in the corner with superhero sheets and blankets, sports posters of the New York Yankees and Dallas Cowboys and sporting paraphernalia scattered in the closet, and a partially built Lego castle on a desk in the other corner with minifigures lying in disarray around the drawbridge. The Lego castle is a perfect time capsule for what happened—one minute everything is fine (depending on your perspective) and the next minute, you stop building your castle and everyone falls down.

Eve and I go back downstairs and sit on the couches in the family room. We've both taken to reading in the mornings there, with the strong sun coming through the front windows of the house. She picks up her book on hand-to-hand combat written by a former Navy SEAL instructor. I open mine, too, but I don't really see any of the words on the page about corn farming. I'm too distracted by what has happened—we added a roommate; we found out the zombies are a lot smarter than expected; and I'm sure this isn't the end of upsetting the applecart. It doesn't seem like too long ago I was in the house by myself, making simple plans (or not). And now, here I am with roommates, a huge problem with the zombie horde, and a ticking clock. I'd like to think this is as crazy as it's going to get, but I'm not that stupid.

I'm right, unfortunately.

That evening is strangely normal, not in the current state, but rather like before. We all kind of wander into the kitchen area around dinnertime, look at each other, and then make drinks. I have to say, I miss two things at this time of day: ice and beer. Warm beer is nasty, foamy, and heavy; I've tried having a few over the past months, but I can't get more than halfway through a can or bottle before I lose interest. Never being a wine drinker, I've skipped raiding the wine cellars during my scouting trips across the neighborhood, so I'm mostly left with the hard stuff. At least mixers are still "good," so we're all drinking room-temperature whiskey tonics.

However, this might not have been a good idea. Whiskey hits me like a freight train and puts me in something of a ready-to-fight mood, whether physically or verbally. I know this, so I'm taking it very easy with the sauce as I warm a few cans of soup (again) over the grill burner. I enjoy the smell of the beef in the stew heating and wonder if the zombies notice cooking smells and whether any of them are taking this in with mouths watering. I hope they're starving and miserable.

The women are inside, and I watch them through the sliding glass doors. DeeDee has also gotten cleaned up since her delivery. It was the same routine as before but with three instead of two while she bathed in the pond. She kept up a running dialogue while she scrubbed, telling us more about her background. I wasn't really surprised when she rattled off how she was a former hostess, bartender, and many other things. No family that she had been in contact with, and she was an actual Huntersville native, which was perhaps even more rare than a Charlotte native. What is additionally surprising is her age. She is just twenty-nine years old. My first guess had been way off, but now that she's cleaned up and a little rested—not to mention loosened up by the drinks—her appearance has softened.

I can't help but notice she's more attractive than I'd given her credit for, nor can I miss how she apparently continues to forgo a bra, as the sun is behind her and the silhouette of her chest is outlined through her thin shirt. That being said, the map of a hard-lived life is etched clearly on her face, with more wrinkles than you'd expect for someone in their late twenties and the residue of excessive tanning and/ or sun exposure weighing on her skin. And, you know, the whole zombie thing.

Anyway, we eat, watch the lingering, Carolina sun burn its way down over the lines of pine trees on the horizon, and then go to bed—alone, all of us.

CHAPTER 10

I wake up very early the next morning to a quiet house and the first glimpse of dawn creeping into the sky. The situation weighs heavily on me, and I find myself very restless. We're terribly outnumbered, basically trapped inside our compound—unless we simply run to a random somewhere since in theory, mankind needs a new place to start if we're "it"—and I have two women living with me.

I'm once again having to ask myself if we have an obligation to repopulate the earth. Eve can't have kids—*at least, she says can't; you don't know if she's telling the truth, amigo*—DeeDee apparently has crotch critters, and above all that, I have a sense of decency with female relations that date back to my teenage years. I've always waited for the woman to kiss me first so that I felt comfortable knowing she was comfortable and was doing what she wanted to do. I'm sure that over the early years in particular, when hormones raged in teenage bodies, I'd made some girls nuts, wondering if I was ever going to make a move. I've just always felt better with my slow approach than being overly assertive.

The way I look at it, if anything does happen between the three of us, then it will be more likely with Eve since my interest in crotch critters is right up there with wanting to French kiss the zombie queen. But, I'm also not sure I'm ready for the complications I'm certain will follow if relationships beyond roommates make their way into the picture.

Sudden outside noise drags me out of the depths of my musings, and I look out the window to see what's going on. When what to my … Oh wait, different story.

They're back—the queen, her minions, her monsters, the whole kit and caboodle.

They have another female. This one looks younger than Eve and DeeDee, at least from where I'm kneeling on the couch. Are the zombies accelerating their searches?

Maybe they're getting better at them too. They're smart in a fucked-up-zombie kind of way and you know it. You're sitting on your ass and doing nothing, comfortable in your little house in your little life of inertia with your two little gal pals. How's that going to work out for you long term, exactly? Got a real plan yet?

I creep out the door and down to the gate, not bothering with an extra gun this time. I know the drill by now. The mob shuffles to a stop in front of me, and I get a closer look at the girl, which is what she is. Middle teens but well into puberty and developed like a young woman. She's carrying the muscular bulk of an athlete in her legs and shoulders. As expected, though, she looks like she's thinner now than she was in the old days. Raven-black hair stops just at her shoulders and is tousled from the march up the street.

She isn't resisting as much as the other women did, but I can see the fear in her dark eyes as they dart everywhere. A Panthers jersey is drooping off one shoulder, and she's wearing turquoise shorts and black running shoes.

They push her forward, but she stops halfway between me and the zombies, arms wrapping around her body and head on a swivel as she looks around nervously. I realize I'm just in a pair of shorts, and given my size and post-death-of-the-world build, I probably look intimidating too.

"It's okay. Come over here. You're safe," I say with a gesture for her to come along. She pauses again, but makes the same decision as the others—human is better than a pack of zombies. I can see her shaking as she comes toward me. She slides behind me and looks over my shoulder.

"What do they want? What's going on?" she asks in a trembling voice.

"You'll see, but don't pay any attention to what happens next. They're not in charge, and there are more people in the house behind the fence. Two women," I add, trying to reassure her. My experience with teenage girls is limited to when I was a teenage boy, and today's kids are different than we were. At least, that's what I assume based on what I read in the news and see around the swimming pools by the clubhouse.

The queen surprises me by not bothering with the babies, food, and more, mime act this time. She just glares at me from under the filthy curtain of hair skewing across her forehead. I'm relieved since I'll have less explaining to do to an already frightened girl. Instead of the old song and dance, the queen moves toward the two of us and reaches for my arm. I stiffen and wish I had that extra gun. Though, if I did have it, I'd blow her head off, and that would be the end since there is no escaping the horde of forty or more zombies behind her.

Her fingers close with stunning speed on my left bicep before I can pull back. With an iron grip, she turns me around and pushes me toward the girl until we're face-to-face. She puts her other hand on the girl's lower back and pushes her until we're uncomfortably mashed together. I'm at least a foot taller than the girl and aware that, despite the athletic muscle development, she's very petite in frame. I marvel grudgingly at the zombie's strength and tell myself to wait because if she's going to hurt me, she's had plenty of chances to do so before now. There's a message here; it's just going to take some figuring out.

"*Bay ... Bay ... ,*" she croaks. She can talk or sort of talk. My head spins. All the others have never done anything other than groan or shout out *Muuuuuuuhhhhh!* whenever they get close to something to eat. Is she evolving? She's searching for women, controlling the rest of the zombies, and not deteriorating like the others. This is horrible. I feel my skin crawl under her clutching hand. I want to pull away. She clearly senses that and tightens her grip.

"*Bay ... Bay ...* " She says this with something of a sigh since the whole word is not coming.

That's what you get for eating people and babies, bitch.

The girl is looking around in confusion, thankfully missing the message but still obviously terrified. I just nod and make what I hope are reassuring sounds. Finally, we're released. I step between the zombie and the girl, trying desperately to control both my anger and fear. I then move in close before saying anything.

"I'm going to kill you. Not today and maybe not tomorrow, but I am going to kill you and kill you slowly. I'll be the last thing you ever see right before you die for good," I promise in an angry whisper. Loathing for this abominable creature washes over me in a flood of hot rage. I think the old "rule" about zombies is that they don't feel pain. Maybe that's true now that they've turned out to be real, but I still plan on finding out. Killing this monster slowly is mostly for my own benefit anyway.

She shakes her head and narrows her eyes. We're adversaries, we both know it, but we also need each other. She's using me to get what she wants since I'm the only male around, and I'm using her to preserve the peace—and now three other lives—until I get a better idea. One of those is going to be undone, and I'm becoming less certain I'm going to be the one left standing at the end of the day. The odds are bad. They're smart, and now I have dependents I can't even list on my tax return.

She breaks eye contact slowly and with arrogance in her expression. She then moves back down the street like before. I want to shout after her that she's brought me three women who cannot give her what she wants—one who can't have children, one who has a non-zombie-related infection, and one who is a child herself—but think better of it since the new girl has no clue what's going on.

I turn back to the girl, say to come inside, and open the gate. As we walk up the driveway to the front porch, I see Eve and DeeDee standing and watching us come closer, mouths agape. They've seen the whole thing or enough of it to feel the same as I do.

This is how we get Amelie.

CHAPTER 11

Knowing it's probably pointless but wanting to retain the sense of caution that has kept me alive thus far, I have the women check the girl for bites in the other room. I'm paranoid, but there is a limit (shocker) to how much of an asshole I can be. I know they'll be thorough and will explain why we have to do this to her. I can hear the girl crying and asking questions while the women try to soothe her. They all come out a few minutes later, with DeeDee's arm around the newcomer. We make introductions all around, and then we learn more about Amelie.

She used to live in the neighborhood with her parents, though they had divorced and lived in separate homes within a few streets of one another. They're gone. No siblings. She's a volleyball player, a setter, fourteen years old but about to turn fifteen in a few weeks—if I can keep us all alive that long. She likes history, *loves* One Direction, doesn't like Justin Bieber because she thinks he's been acting totally stupid just to stay famous, wants a red convertible car, and misses her dogs.

It's a little dizzying hearing a random stream of consciousness come from her based on what she's been through just now and over the prior months. But kids are more resilient than adults, and we're also, apparently, the first people she's seen since the world crashed. She has a lot to get off her chest.

Amelie has survived much like the rest of us—hiding in houses, eating cold food when she could find it, and sleeping when she could or when she just ran out of steam. She was caught in the same manner as DeeDee and Eve too—they searched for and found her over the course of a couple of days before finally cornering and capturing her this morning.

Starving like the others had been, we set about feeding her and giving her something to drink—no whiskey for this one, though she probably deserves one or two. DeeDee takes the lead in feeding her and rubbing her back while she demolishes two cans of ravioli and several bottles of water.

CHAPTER 12

More settling into the routine of life as it has come to be. The house is starting to feel full, though, I don't mind the constant hubbub of background noise as the women get to know one another. The silence of the past few months now looms over me and makes me feel odd about not finding people sooner. I recognize that there may have been too much silence in my life even before everything went boom. I often find myself just sitting with a book in my lap but not reading, just listening to what passes for the new normal.

DeeDee has really taken Amelie under her wing; they're attached at the hip as we go through our next few days. Not that Eve doesn't get along with them, but the other two seem to have formed a quick, tight bond. Frankly, I'm surprised it's DeeDee, but there is plenty of room in my mind for what could be versus what had been.

Since DeeDee arrived, Eve stopped her occasional forays into my room at night without explanation. I understand. Easy to make assumptions.

I'm fighting sleep (mostly unsuccessfully) on the fifth night after Amelie joined us when I hear the bedroom door slip open, bringing me out of the heavy fog of near-sleep. I'm expecting Eve, but it isn't her.

"Hi," she says. It's DeeDee. "Can I come in? Eve told me she came in to sleep next to you sometimes, and she thought it'd be okay with you if I did."

She stands in the doorway, with one hand on the knob and one on the door frame. The past few weeks have been good to her, softening the lines around her eyes and putting a few pounds back on her slender frame. With the moonlight shining on her through the windows that bracket my bed, I can't help but notice she's (as always) not wearing anything under her shirt—it's impossible to miss that part of her. And when you come down to it, she's a very attractive woman, just one with some tough miles from life on her.

I simply nod, still dragging myself fully awake. I then actually say the word "yes" since there's no way she could have seen the nod in the dark.

Sliding into the bed on the side nearest to the window, she snuggles in close to me.

Unlike Eve, she faces me and even drapes an arm across my bare chest. She tucks in tight as she settles. I can smell the shampoo in her hair and the soap on her skin. Part of me is *very* aware of the physical contact. I try awfully hard to think about baseball, zombies, anything else to keep things quiet. I'm not sure that's going to work since the longer she lies on my side the more aware I become of her right breast (and perky nipple!) pushing into my ribs. *Jesus.*

"Thanks," she whispers. "I don't want anything. Well, unless you do. This is a lonely new world, and I've always had a man in my life and bed. I think old habits are hard to break, but this isn't about old habits. You're nice, and you've been good to all of us. Even without this fort and the food and stuff, I think you're a good person. I haven't met too many of those lately, or ever."

I don't know what to say or do, but I know one thing I am *not* going to do—that will complicate the dynamic in the house. I don't want to be the cause of that, no matter what. Also, there's the infamous crotch critters to consider.

As if reading my mind, she speaks up. "You know, I was joking about the crotch critters when we met. I didn't know if you were some kind of fucked-up zombie king who was using those god-awful creatures to kidnap a bunch of girls to rape or what. So, I wanted to test you. Funny thing is, you know what you're getting with zombies. But you still probably don't know what you're gonna get with people. So, you know, you don't have to worry about that in case you wanna, you know, do something more than sleep."

Oh boy. She's right, though, on that point—the zombies are at least consistent or have been until they started delivering women to my doorstep. They chase you and try to eat you; you fight back and kill them. Pretty simple new world when you think about it. People are a mess.

"I think this is about second chances, if we can survive those monsters," she continues. "People had the world kinda messed up before all this. If you believed in God, it was starting to get easy to think he had given up on us. I've been thinkin' maybe this is his new version of the great flood. Wash the world clean and start over, you know?"

"You might be right," I answer. I haven't thought of it like that at all, but I admit to thinking more than once that the new reality isn't necessarily a terrible change in some respects. I do reluctantly notice how I have originally been judging her according to the old rules, thinking a little less of her because of her obviously "bad" background, and I'm immediately contrite. This is about second chances, for all of us. Maybe even me too.

"Let's keep this simple, if that's okay with you. I like you, too, and I'm glad you're with us, me. But, I think this would make things funny in the house, if you know what I mean. Not that Eve and I have anything going—she probably told you that, too," I say and feel her nod in the dark. "But now we have Amelie to think about, too, and she might be confused between the damn zombie bitch's show out in the street and this. I would hate to scare her." I desperately want to kiss and hold DeeDee. The desire for her is raging in me, in all my parts, just wanting to hold someone close and caress her. I want to drown into the embrace and dance in the dark. It's been horribly lonely, and while any affection would be good, DeeDee has a grounded, practical, shoot-from-the-hip honesty that I like. But, I know this is the right decision.

"I'm all right with that. I won't even try to change your mind even though I can tell it wouldn't take much work. Can I still stay?"

"Of course," I reply. I'm never going to get to sleep now, anyway.

She drops off first. I feel and hear her breathing slow down and her body settle into a peaceful sleep beside me. Her head is tucked into my neck, arm still across me, and after a while, her right leg makes its way across my legs too. I lie awake for a long time, thinking about her, second chances, redemption, and how to kill those fucking zombies while keeping all of us alive in the process. It ends up being a long night.

CHAPTER 13

’m awake first, like always, and leave a still-slumbering DeeDee in the bed. In a little sliver of sunlight, I notice a tattooed ankle sticking out from underneath the covers. I tiptoe over and see it's a simple yin-yang tattoo. I wonder if she also has a tramp stamp on her lower back and then immediately chastise myself for being an idiot.

Keep throwing rocks, my friend, since, of course, none of the glass in your house is broken.

It's very early. The watch on the bedside table says it's just past five, though I'm not sure if we've had daylight savings yet or if the clock is even right. Ha. It's going to be weird, though, once all the watch batteries in the world run out. I rarely wear one anyway—there's no need to anymore. No schedule, no need to be anywhere at a particular time. Just go to bed when it's dark, get up when it's light. Simple. But, I might go find a windup watch or a fancy one powered by the sun or kinetic motion or whatever. It's all on sale.

I start making the coffee as quietly as I can, pouring a few bottles of water into a teapot and taking it outside to the grill and its very handy side burner. After grabbing the

French press and mug and setting them onto the patio table, I sit down in one of the wicker chairs to enjoy the view over the golf course. Mist rises from the lake, writhing upward from the brackish water and dissipating as the day warms and comes to life. I can hear various critters stirring—birds chirping to one another as they (probably) enjoy their mostly-human-free day.

The kettle begins to rattle gently on the burner as the water heats. I push myself out of the seat and pick up the mug when I see motion across the sprawling fairway below the house.

Shit.

It's a man running away from a group of zombies. There might be about ten of them in the pack, and from here, it looks like they're gaining on him. I drop the mug onto the deck and it shatters, scattering the handle off to one side. I run into the house and sweep up both .45 handguns from an antique table near the door. I grab the shotgun from an umbrella stand as I go, not taking any care to be quiet as I make it to the front door.

"Eve! DeeDee! Wake up!" I shout at the top of my lungs. "We have a problem!"

Hauling the door wide open and sprinting out and around the wall, I tuck the pistols into my waistband and rack the shotgun to chamber a round. I hope it's a slug and immediately wish I'd brought the rifle. I have the shotguns loaded with alternating slugs and shot, but I can't remember which is first because it's been a while since I've had a fight. From this distance, the shotgun's going to be unreliable. It's too late to turn back now, though. I fight my way through the shrubs bordering the property and golf course and try to spot where the man and zombies are.

They're about 200 yards away from me, just passing the still-standing, 150-yard marker post and coming toward me. The man looks like he's tiring and heavy-footed. As I run to close the distance between us, he staggers and barely catches himself with one hand on the turf. He manages to keep himself upright and moving. The horde is closing on him, no more than twenty feet behind and narrowing the gap steadily. Rather than go directly toward them, I change direction and rush to the side so I can come at them from an angle. I haven't been seen yet, and the straight angle would be poor if I have buckshot in the gun first.

The hard months have been good for me too. I'm in obscene shape and can run like a deer. I haven't been in shape like this since high school. Though I carry a good bit more muscle mass than I did back then. Jumping over a golf bag laying on the course—need to clean that up; it'll kill the grass—I come into the group from ninety degrees and fire the shotgun from the hip at the zombies closest to the front.

Buckshot. It tears the two leading zombies nearly in half, and they go down in a spray of blood and viscera. The man snaps his head toward me in shock. He keeps running, but he angles toward me. I wave him to move to the side, rack another round, and fire again, neatly removing the head of the second-nearest monster with the slug. The body takes another step, pauses, and then tips to the side spewing gore from the neck. The rest of the zombies come to a stumbling halt, some bumping into the others.

There are eight more of them, all male, and all look like "normal" zombies. Not that I can really tell the difference, but none of them look like ones from the pack that have been visiting lately. I wave the shotgun at them, but I wait before pulling the trigger again. Eight is a lot, and they're fairly close, so there's no guarantee I'll be able to kill them all by myself. They glare at me—chests heaving and eyes glowering, angry groans coming out of their drooling maws—but then they turn as one and move away, across the dewy, emerald grass. After watching for a moment to ensure they're really leaving, I finally spin around to get a look at the newest arrival.

CHAPTER 14

I know him; he's a guy from the neighborhood. Right now he's a shaking mess, but I've seen him a number of times around the pool, at the gym, and on the golf course. I don't like him. I don't know him that well, but I've seen enough to not be particularly pleased that he's the one who had to show up.

He was ugly to his family at the pool and a machine hog in the gym, leaving his towel and weights on a bench while jumping on the treadmill for a few minutes before going back, as if he owned the entire place. I've watched him be short with and obnoxious to the staff at the club—always complaining about something with an entitled pout to his face—and improve his lie and "take" six-foot putts as gimmes when he missed them. I've been in his golf group a few times over the past couple years. Not by choice, but only when I didn't have someone to play with and got partnered with his gang.

He's a hail-fellow-well-met, back-slapping jackass who will forget your name ten seconds after being introduced and then call you "buddy" or "pal" throughout the round. And he's a very good golfer, better than me, but he still seems to feel the need to cheat, which I don't understand.

My biggest gripe with him, however, is how he drives. He rolls through every stop sign in the neighborhood at ten miles per hour in his enormous, gleaming, white BMW 7 Series sedan while texting, looking at pictures of Kardashians or whatever or blabbing on the phone. We almost had a run-in at one point when I was out jogging. He nearly hit me because he didn't look in my direction before he swept through a stop. I banged my hand against the side of his car in anger, but he rushed off without stopping.

In short, he embodies a lot of the qualities of what's wrong with the world. In all fairness, none of these things are enough to condemn him, but I know he's a jerk and I'm a little pissed. I can't believe I just saved his life, of all people. But who knows, maybe he's changed, or I got a wrong impression. One can hope.

"Buddy! Thank you, man!" He practically shouts. "They've been chasing me for a half hour. Good thing I'm in such good shape, or they would've caught me." Um, don't forget the guy with the shotgun. I try to channel DeeDee's kind thoughts about second chances.

"I'm Jack," he continues. "We've never met, but I'm glad to see you. What the hell is going on? Do you live around here?" he asks. I see no reason to correct him about our past meetings; there's no point in it, and this is the new world.

I reintroduce myself and then tell him to come along back to the house. All three women are at the gate waiting for us, and I notice DeeDee is carrying the rifle. By the way she's handling it, she looks very comfortable with a long gun. I make a mental note to ask her about it since another capable shooter will be a good thing. Eve goes pale when she gets a good look at Jack. She quickly turns away toward the house and goes straight inside, well ahead of the rest of us.

Following a quick scan of the perimeter to confirm the pack of zombies hasn't changed their minds and is coming back around for seconds, the rest of us trail her to the house after closing the gate.

As we make it through the front door and into the foyer, DeeDee reminds me, "Aren't you going to check him?" Oh boy, this'll be fun. Jack snaps his head around.

"Yeah … Jack, look, you need to strip so we can check you to make sure you're clean from bites," I say reluctantly but with a firm voice since I have a feeling this is not going to go well.

"Are you kidding me?" His voice immediately takes a different tone, with a clear challenge in it. "I'm not taking my clothes off in front of you people."

"Yes, you are. This is not an optional exercise. All of us have been checked since arriving so all of us can remain safe. This is about the group, not you." Well, all of us have been checked except for me, but I know I'm clean. I bring the handgun around from behind my back and vaguely wave it toward him. "I know this is awkward, but this is the way it's gotta be. You can always go back outside and take your chances." I gesture at the front door with the barrel of the gun.

He stares at me. We're about the same size, but he's country club fit, and I'm badass, zombie-killing fit. Not to mention, I have the gun. He's definitely going to be a problem. But, his eyes drop first.

"I run a multimillion-dollar company. Twenty people work for me. I've got the biggest, nicest house in the neighborhood and a brand new, top-end BMW, and some scruffy jackass with a pistol is telling me to take my clothes off," he mumbles. "This is utter bullshit and I'm going to—"

I move quickly, and before he can react or move, I'm right on top of him, very much in his personal space. I watch his eyes dilate as they adjust to the sudden proximity. "You're going to what? Call your lawyer?" I spit. "You *ran* a multi-million-dollar company. Twenty people *worked* for you, and now they're all dead. Your big, nice house is probably full of zombies or wild animals, and your stop-sign-running BMW is collecting dust as we speak. All that shit is in the past, so get with the goddamn program and wake up. This is a new world, and I just saved your ass. Take your damn clothes off, show us that ass, and let's get this over with."

I tell the women to go into a different room and he disrobes, glaring at me the whole time. I've just made him look bad in front of the women and have won the initial pissing contest, so I know this isn't really over. After checking him quickly but thoroughly, I tell him to get dressed, glad it's over.

"Are you a fag? Did you get a good look? I saw you check my package. If you're like that, you better tell me now since I'm not that way."

"I have to check everything on everyone. Grow up."

Kill him. Do it.

No, he's a human being. Though I have a feeling that the more we get to know him, the more I'll regret not listening to the voice inside my head. I close my anger down, try to remain civil, and usher him into the kitchen.

We make introductions—to which he pays little attention—and give him some food and water. Eve remains on the fringes of the conversation, glancing at him from behind Amelie's shoulder. She's clearly troubled by his presence.

"Don't you have anything better than soup? I'm starving and haven't eaten in two days," he complains. I roll my eyes, inside my head mind you.

"Sorry, *buddy*. That's what we've got," I reply. "Slim pickings these days."

He rolls his eyes—outside his head, of course—and then bends back to his meal. I study him as he does so. The sweat from running away from the zombies is still visible on his forehead, and his shirt is drenched. I notice it's a very expensive golf shirt; he also has on a good pair of khakis and high-end running shoes. He's a good-looking man with dark hair and frosty blue eyes underneath a broad face. I guess he's right around forty, but he may be younger or older by a couple years. Big through the chest, even after everyone's forced diet, and overall well-muscled in a country-club kind of way. I carry a raggedy semibeard since it doesn't seem to be much of a priority these days, but he's actually clean-shaven. I try to wrap my mind around someone who's so fastidious as to find newish clothes and keep himself groomed, but I find that I cannot.

Jack finishes his meal and looks around at our group after carefully wiping his mouth on a paper towel. His eyes linger on DeeDee's torso a little longer than I like and then does the same to Amelie. Yeah, he's a jerk.

"So what's the story here?" he asks. "Are you all some kind of family? I don't recognize any of you, and I know this isn't your house since I knew the people who lived here before. David was a good guy and a sick golfer. He had a two handicap, man. And his wife, whew, she was a real looker. What an ... " He stops himself and then shakes his head at the memory, but I wonder if it's for the man or for the wife.

"Wait a second. Eve, is that you?" He pops up on his toes in an attempt to get a better look at Eve, who's still mostly hidden behind Amelie. "It is you! Oh my God! You made it. You're alive. Hey," he pauses and cocks his head to one side. "You still owe me one, right?" He laughs, not kindly. Eve pales even further than her natural coloring, if that's possible, and says nothing.

"Did you guys steal this house?"

Seriously? "Steal" a house, in *this* situation? I feel myself bristling. My thoughts flit to the idea of taking him outside and either shooting him or calling all the zombies back to finish the job.

Do it, do it, do it. He's an asshole and is going to cause problems. Just shoot him. The girls won't care. I bet they won't hold it against you or look at you differently.

Sure they won't.

I push the thoughts away and explain how I've come to get the house. He shrugs, but looks at me strangely, studying me. I wonder if he recognizes me from golf or around the clubhouse, but then he proves that thought wrong.

"I guess it's okay. Not like they need the house. You all can live here. It's no big deal since I knew them." Oh goodie. We get permission! There's a petulant look on his face I really, really don't like.

Doitdoitdoitdoit.

I leave the room and go out front, excusing myself on the way, saying I'm going to check for zombies again. These new ones bother me—we've been living in relative quiet over the past few weeks, without any attacks or really any sightings once I made the "deal" with queenie. If there are rogue groups out there, too, we have to be even more careful than we have already been. Lovely.

As I move through the house, I can hear DeeDee start to give Jack an explanation of what has brought us all together. Several seconds after I close the front door, Eve follows me out. The fingers of her right hand are up close to her mouth, as if she's been chewing her fingernails. The peaceful weeks have been good for her too. She has more weight on her and is far more relaxed than she has been. I know she feels safe here, but she's also clearly bothered by Jack's arrival.

"What's up?" I ask. "You don't look happy."

"I shouldn't say anything," she pauses, probably thinking some of the same things I've been. He's another person after all.

"Yes, you should. If you know something important then you need to share it so we'll all know. We're together in this, and we have to be on the same page so we can all stay safe."

Eve works a finger in the corner of her mouth, nibbling on the edge. "I know him. *We* knew them. I was friendly with his wife from book club," she begins, halts, and then resumes. "He's a jerk. Definitely not a good person. We went to their house one New Year's Eve a couple years ago, and he hit on me."

"Okay. Though not great, that's not too shocking. But, you know, everyone's drinking too much on New Year's. Plus, you're attractive, so I can see it happening." When I say she's attractive, her eyes flick up to meet mine briefly.

"No, I know stuff like that happens and I get it. It was the way he went about it that scared me."

Scared her? Super—this is going to just keep on getting better, isn't it? I tell her to go on.

"He followed me when I went to the bathroom. I didn't know he had, so I didn't lock the door. Plus, I was a little drunk. Right after I slid my pants down and was about to sit, he walked right in as if I'd invited him. He was staring down at … you know. I actually apologized for not locking the door and asked him to leave. He didn't, though, and just kept staring at me. Then he pulled his thing out and waved it at me, saying he knew I wanted it. He came over to grab the back of my head and pulled me toward him." This all comes out in a tumble and tears are sliding down her cheeks as she speaks.

"He's much bigger than me, and I didn't know what to do. Scream? My husband works … *worked* for him. That would have been a big mess, so I told him I was on my period. He said he wasn't interested in that, just a blowjob would be good enough, and wasn't I thankful for the nice dinner and evening? Wasn't I grateful for the good job my husband had so we could afford nice things, all thanks to him? He said I should show my appreciation, and we'd keep it our 'little New Year's secret.'" Her voice is shaking, and I move over toward her, not sure whether I'm supposed to hug her or something like that, but she holds up a hand.

"Nothing ended up happening since one of the other people at the party came bouncing down the hallway, looking for the bathroom. But I never forgot that. I was humiliated and felt violated, as if something more had happened. For a while, I even felt guilty and ashamed, like it was my fault he did that to me. I loathe that man." I admit, I like the anger I see in her eyes. I think Eve is tougher than she realizes.

"Ever since then, every time he sees me, he says the same damn thing: 'You still owe me one, right?' It makes me sick to my stomach. I hate him, and I don't want to be in the same house as him." The tears have dried up, replaced by her anger. I want to hug her just for that. We need anger, and I don't want her knocked down by this clown. *Sorry, clowns, that's probably unfair to you.*

"Okay," I say. "Thanks for telling me. We'll have to keep an eye on him. If anything happens, let me know, and I'll handle it if you want, in any way you want. I don't like him either due to some past experiences, though nothing like that, but it's not like we can kick him out." Though if I'm being honest with myself, I'm already kind of hoping for an excuse to do just that.

For a few moments, she seems to be deciding about whether to disagree with that last statement, but then she nods. She keeps her head down as we go back inside. I pat her gently on the shoulder as she passes me.

And now we're a handful.

CHAPTER 15

The next few days go by slowly, with a new feeling of unease smothering the house. Jack's arrival and behavior has unsettled all of us, and the house is beginning to feel really small. All the supplies and weapons I've gathered have taken over a few rooms, which puts Jack on the couch (endless complaints) and the rest of us in bedrooms. Too bad—he should've showed up earlier. Of course, I probably would've kicked him out of a room once another female showed up anyway so she'd have better privacy.

He's such a pain. He constantly challenges me, doesn't like the way we do things, hates the couch, and says the house is too small. It has become almost impossible for me to not just give in to the voice inside my head and either shoot him or vote him out of the house, but I try to be decent.

"Why don't we have a generator running?" he asks. He's seen it out back. It's plugged in and everything, so he doesn't understand why we can't run it and have the lights on at night, cook warm food indoors, and so on. The fact of the matter is, I connected it once before, but the sounds made the zombies batshit crazy for some reason. They wandered around the perimeter, moaning and bumping into the walls. So, for the sake of getting some rest, I shut it down. Besides, I really don't mind living without it. We get along fine in the evenings with candles and some kerosene lanterns I've come across in my shopping trips—though he whines about the smell of the kerosene—and cooking on the side burner of the grill is fine. Hot food is hot food regardless of how it gets hot, in my opinion, but he's a chronic pain in the ass. Of course, he can't be bothered to help with cooking or cleaning. He basically sits around and does as little as possible to contribute, but he keeps a running criticism going of just about everything.

One thing is bubbling up along the way, nudging a vague thought into my mind, though I can't quite grasp it. It's like hitting the driver straight; it always just eludes me—except on the last round that had been all right with driver for the most part until I mashed it on eighteen; at least it mashed into one of those gelatinous bastards. Something about how everyone had been pursued?

So, I ask Jack how he ran into the pack of zombies chasing him, and he says he'd gone back to his old house in the far-back reaches of the neighborhood to get something. But when he got there late in the evening, all the zombies were out together in the middle of the cul-de-sac he lived on. They were huddled around a single female zombie in the center. He watched them for a few minutes, knowing he couldn't get any closer or go into his house. He was fascinated and watched her gesture to small groups. When she pointed them in varying directions, they departed in waves. Not all of them left; there was a small group with two big zombies and several ordinary ones who stayed behind with the female. Out of sheer coincidence, they all went into his house. He crept away and went into a different house nearby rather than find his way back through the hunting packs to his other hiding spot. When he woke up the next morning, he collided with a group of zombies who pursued him until he reached us.

That clarifies and confirms how Eve, DeeDee, and Amelie had been found. The queen is sending out organized search parties to find and bring people back to "our" group. I think long and hard about the fact that they're all clustered together in a single place, but I can't find the answer in my mind. I let it go in the hopes that something will just come to me.

I resume packing things into the garage to get ready for leaving. New York is the destination since it's much closer than Colorado. Plus, I lived there for most of my formative years. I know both how to get there and how to get around once arriving. And there isn't going to be as much wide-open space between cities and towns on the way to New York. I want to be able to resupply along the way as needed.

I know that's the right thing to do, just go and get away from the zombie mob, or at least this one. I'm worried, however, that there may be many, many more of them elsewhere, and I wonder if it's better to stay put and deal with the devil I know. There's the question of Jack and whether I can stand being cooped up in a vehicle with him for a long period of time. I think it would be unfair to make him ride in the bed, though it's an appealing compromise to me anyway.

Part of my hesitation is that I desperately want to kill the zombie queen and all her followers. I also know this area and am not in a hurry for change that may lead to something worse. The thought that they may be evolving into something more dangerous than they already are and that she may be the linchpin of their evolution—and therefore, the key to stopping it—makes me want to end her in a big way. No matter what, I know we're running out of time. It's been a while since we've had a visit, so I'm sure we're due any day now for a status check.

It's getting hotter too. The idea of getting out of the sunny south and the forthcoming, sweltering late spring and early summer weather is beginning to weigh on my mind. Not that New York will be pleasant in the winter, but we can be modern day snowbirds if we have to—shuttling between whatever there is in New York and then back here or somewhere else for the winter months. Regardless, the status quo is not going to work anymore. I keep packing, debating the ideas in my mind, and generally trying to stay busy so I can avoid the growing tension in the house.

CHAPTER 16

A few days later, Eve and DeeDee come to me, finding me in the garage as I pour gas stabilizer into the jerrycans I've accumulated. I know nothing about the shelf life of gasoline other than you're supposed to put some stabilizer into your tanks and fill your lawnmower to the brim once you finish the final cut for the year. My plan is to stop whenever needed and refuel from gas stations, but having backup plans has been good thus far. I'm a creature of habit if nothing else.

Eve speaks up first. "We need to go shopping, please, to a store and not a nearby house. We just need a change of pace, something different to do. We're cooped up and have been confined to the house for weeks. We've just kind of been sitting and waiting for something to happen. Not to mention him ... " She trails off.

"Shopping for what?" I ask. "We've pretty much got everything we need, don't we?"

"We do," DeeDee jumps in. "But, Eve and I, we need to get some female garments, if you follow."

I don't and shake my head in response. DeeDee continues to come into my room to sleep from time to time, and Eve is starting to come again as well. Luckily, they must have worked out some kind of system since there's never been an evening where they both arrive at the same time. That would probably be the last straw in my willpower since, really, who doesn't dream about that? Well, what *guy* doesn't dream about that, anyway? Unless one or both of them have some ideas about enhancing the relationship, I have no clue what kind of female garments they require.

"It's bras we need. We both want new ones, not ones that someone else has worn—that's kind of creepy," DeeDee explains. "You know neither one of us wears one, but neither one of us likes the way that Jack looks at us. He stares. All the time. Eve told me about what happened back in the day with him. Makes me shiver, I tell you." She gives an exaggerated shake as she finishes. "Me, I don't like 'em, and Eve here doesn't really need one, like you know, but he's gonna burn a hole in my shirt starin' at my nipples. I know you sneak a peek here and there and that's okay. I know you don't mean nothing by it, and they *are* kind of hard to miss and all, but that man makes me feel dirty."

Eve nods in agreement.

I desperately hope I'm not as red in the face as I suspect I may be. DeeDee's right—it's hard to avoid admiring her physique from time to time. I can't believe she knows, but that's a mistake men have been making since the first woman turned up.

"Okay, we can do that, I guess. Do you think Amelie needs one too?" I ask. Since I didn't take part in checking her, I don't know what she needs in that area. However, I suspect she's all set since a middle teen is unlikely to forego a bra, and she's a little curvy. I'm not blind. Plus, we're all practically living on top of each other.

They shake their heads in tandem.

I ponder what to do. Do we all go, which will let Jack know, once they pick up the bras, that he has made the adult women uncomfortable and, therefore, gives a 'point'? Do I just take the three women and leave him behind so he can get into unknown mischief? I don't like the idea of leaving him alone in the house. His demeanor is miserable. I know he dislikes me as much as I do him, and I assume it's only a matter of time before we have a come-to-Jesus moment that may get messy. Giving him a window to plot and arrange that seems like a poor strategy. But maybe with a task to accomplish, something that makes him feel valued and important, he'll start to turn the corner?

We decide just the three of us will go but only to the nearby superstore a few miles down the road as opposed to a much larger mall several more miles away. The superstore is within walking distance, technically, and I would enjoy the exercise. However, there are the rogue zombies who chased Jack to consider, and we may see other things we'll benefit from gathering once there. With that in mind, we decide to take the truck. It's better for disposing of streetwalking zombies too.

I stroll through the house and find Jack. I explain what we're going to do and ask him if he needs us to pick anything up for him. He shakes his head, clearly unhappy with the idea of being left out. The former master of the universe has reverted to childish behavior.

"Jack, I need you to stay here so you can watch the house and keep an eye on Amelie. You know, keep her safe, make sure the gate's closed behind us. We need someone to watch things while we go out and know you're the guy for the job." I laugh inside since he's the *only* guy, but why call that out? "We know we can rely on you," I add.

He perks up a bit at that. He nods and says he'll be glad to. His mood seems to lift significantly, and I think it's because he'll be out from under my feet and have the place mostly to himself. Maybe, he just needs something to do, and this will do the trick temporarily. The three of us get into the truck, pull out through the gate, and pause to watch him close it behind us. He grins and waves a little as he shuts it. I still feel uneasy, but I know we won't be gone for very long. I'm going to push the girls to make it quick. At least we don't have to wait in long checkout lines.

CHAPTER 17

ll of us are armed, me with the shotgun and KNIFE (that will never get old) and both women with the pair of .45 handguns. It begins as an uneventful trip; it's easy enough to force the electronic doors open. A crowbar has been one of my best friends in the preceding months. Simple, elegant in a rudimentary way, unchanged for many moons, and very effective at what it's designed to do, including some things its manufacturers never dreamed of, like whacking zombies over the head and sending them to the ground in a hurry. No surprises from critters in aisle three as we enter—guess they don't have crowbars—though we do find a couple of very ripe, human corpses in the electronics area clutching iPods and Nintendo DSs. The odor is overwhelming, and we move quickly away, thankful it's far from the women's area.

After swooping up a couple carts, the women make fairly quick work of it, gathering some brassieres from the petite and slutty, ex-stripper sections. Just kidding. Eve keeps things simple, finding a couple sports bras rather quickly and going into a changing room to put one on.

I spend my time scanning the store visually and listening carefully for any disturbances. I look out over the kids' clothes, racy women's undergarments—I mean, is some of that stuff for real?—sporting goods, and so on. I run my fingers over some of the men's clothing, idly thinking about how Jack's wardrobe is so much nicer than mine despite the availability of endless wearables in my size. I grab a couple shirts and place them in our cart. I hear Eve and DeeDee chatting on as they shop, likely about all the same things women used to talk about in this store and others. I find myself happy to hear their voices sound perkier than they have recently. If nothing else, we all needed to get out of the house.

"How about this, y'all?"

I hear DeeDee's voice from behind me and foolishly turn around to see her standing outside the dressing room in a demi-cup, black lace bra that covers maybe half of her boobs and a matching pair of boy short-type bottoms. She rests one hand on her hip, which is cocked just so. She looks spectacular in a spectacular way, curves bursting out in all directions.

I tear my eyes off her and try to focus on my visual patrol of the store, with little luck. Her next nighttime visit is going to be torture since there's no way I'm going to get this image of her out of my head. Nor, I admit, do I want to. This is far different from when she had to strip at delivery; that had been nearly clinical, while this is just riveting with everything (mostly) covered but also visible enough to blow my mind.

I hear her giggle and say to Eve, "I guess he approves, huh?" Eve titters and says maybe she should get something fancy too. I know they're having fun at my expense, but it's a good fun reflecting their improved mood. This isn't going to solve our problems, but sometimes laughter really is the best medicine. I smile for the first time in a long time.

We finish collecting a few more things, including some clothes the girls think Amelie will like, and head back out to the truck.

CHAPTER 18

The trip has taken maybe an hour at most. I usually wear a watch, but I had left it at home after bathing in the pond. I've made this same trip endless times in the past, though, so I have a good idea of how long it took, especially without having to wait for traffic and stoplights. We coast to a stop outside the gate at the foot of the driveway. While I do a quick scan around the edges of the property, Eve drives the truck through and parks. The girls unload their conquests and chat gaily with each other as I go up to the door and open it.

The house is quiet.

Too quiet.

I wave at the girls to tell them to be silent. I then bring the shotgun to the ready, gesturing for them to put their bags down and be prepared.

Fearing the utter worst and moving slowly through the foyer, I come into the kitchen. Still no sounds, no smells, nothing at all. I carefully sweep into the kitchen and family room area and then notice the French door that leads off to the deck is ajar. I head silently toward it. I feel more than hear the women come into the room, so I signal for them to stay put as I creep to the doorframe.

Thankfully, I hear voices, both Jack's and Amelie's, murmuring just on the fringes of earshot. I breathe a sigh of relief and then gently open the door enough for me to squeeze through. I stop, curious to hear what they're saying. From what I've seen thus far, Jack's had little interest in Amelie besides telling her to get him things as if she's his own kid. Otherwise, he's usually ignoring her as he does with the rest of us, with the exception of ogling the adult women.

"…but this is what we need to do," I hear Jack say. "Those zombies are going to all come and get us and kill us if we don't have babies. No matter how many guns we have or how tough he thinks he is, how are we going to fight off all of them?" Guess that's me he's talking about.

He continues. "He even told me to have this talk with you while they were all gone. He said he was too afraid to tell you. You know he's having sex with both Eve and DeeDee, right? They go into his room just about every night, and I bet you they're both pregnant by now. He wants us to have sex, too, so we can make babies for those monsters and all be safe." I rage inside as I hear this. I want to run outside, point the shotgun at the back of his head, and blow his brains across the backyard in a beautiful spatter. My grip on the gun tightens and I wait.

Amelie sniffs and says, "I don't know. I'm only fourteen. I've never even fooled around with a boy. I've heard girls at school talk about it, and my cousin says … said that it hurts a lot." I can hear her crying softly, which somehow balances and fuels my anger. I'm going to kill this man.

"But we have to, don't you see? They're going to kill us otherwise. This is what the others want, but they just weren't brave enough to tell you themselves. I'll be really gentle, I promise. Let's go inside while they're gone. We can do it in your room. It's okay—it'll be good. You'll like it."

"I guess so," she snuffles. "If it's what everyone wants."

My hands grip the stock of the shotgun to the point where the wood creaks. I'm beyond furious, and now I want to kill him with my bare hands. He must have heard the sound because his head swivels toward the door. I duck quickly back out of his line of sight and turn to see DeeDee and Eve still standing quietly with questioning looks on their faces. I usher them back out the front door and quickly explain in hushed tones what I overheard. I also tell them I'm going to kill him, right now. They're both stunned and horrified. DeeDee looks like she agrees with me and is maybe going to march inside and take care of him herself. Surprisingly, it's Eve who comes to his defense.

"You can't kill him now, not in front of her," Eve urges. "Amelie won't understand anything other than that you've lost it. She'll be confused by what he said and what you did and might even think it's her fault or that you're trying to keep all of us just for yourself. Why don't you take him away and talk to him, scare him or something? We'll talk to her, explain what's going on, and clear things up. He's still a person," she adds, grudgingly.

I think it through and decide she's right. For Amelie's sake, he gets to live another day, but we're going to straighten everything out once and for all. We quietly go back into the house. We make it to the family room just in time to see him leading her to the foot of the stairs to the second floor. The look on his face says it all—guilt, shock, and disappointment are written all over it. I hope I'll be able to keep my cool. It isn't going to be easy. All the problems he has brought into the house, all the things that bothered me about him beforehand, and now all these lies in order to coerce a child into having sex with him. It's all overwhelming my sense of decency.

"Jack, we're going for a ride," I say with as much calm as I can muster. "We need to go pick up some heavy things from the store that I couldn't get with the ladies. I need someone stronger to help me." Amelie looks at me, and I notice it's differently than how she used to look at me. There's some measure of distrust. My anger grows. I leave the room and slowly put the shotgun back into the umbrella rack. I need to get it out of my hands.

He hesitates, likely guessing this is a ruse but acknowledging his little tryst is not to be. Therefore, there's no good reason for him to refuse. Shrugging, he turns to Amelie and says they'll "talk more later" and then heads toward the front door, brushing against me as he goes past. I glance at the women, who both nod with cautioning looks on their faces, silently telling me to keep him alive. I sweep the keys to the Challenger off the counter, wanting something different to drive than the truck and needing to vent somehow; it's the perfect car for that. As I pass DeeDee, I take the .45 from her left hand and snug it into the back of my shorts, draping my shirt over the top of it.

Jack stops in the driveway, unsure of which vehicle we're going to take and probably whether I have any idea of what he was trying to do with Amelie. I gesture to the Challenger, and he gives me a confused look.

"I thought you said we have to pick up heavy things? Don't we need the truck?" he asks.

"Just get in the car."

"But why? I don't like this car. It's too loud. I want to take the truck," he complains.

Some things never change.

"Jack, get in the car now, or I'm going to shoot you in the knee, throw you into the car, and we'll be on our way whether you like it or not." With that, he quickly goes over to the passenger side and climbs in. I open the gate, get into the car, and turn the key fob. The beast thunders to life, shattering the quiet of the neighborhood as I goose the throttle. I slip the gearshift to neutral, coast back out of the driveway onto the street, and set the parking brake.

After closing the gate, I stop to look at and listen to the car for a moment. It wasn't my car when everything went down, but rather it was one I had acquired during my rounds of accumulation. Black paint, black interior, tinted windows, R/T model with 376-horsepower and a 6-speed stick. There were a few of the SRT8 models on the Dodge dealer's lot, too, which are notably faster, but after driving both of them, I decided I liked the "slower" model. It's better for comfort, handling, and cruising around. And the SRT8 models either had obnoxious colors or had various stripes and stickers scattered across the sheet metal, which is not to my liking. Hard to argue with a simple, black muscle car.

There are some dents and dings in it from various encounters with zombies on the roads over the past months. Sometimes it's just easier to bump them with the side of the car than get out and use up ammunition. Before all my roommates arrived, I'd cleared out three of them while I was driving (fooling around) on a dirt road on the outskirts of town and drifting sideways through a turn. They were nicely aligned across the road, and the car wiped them out in one fell swoop. Not great for the paint, and the car is starting to look like it belongs in a postapocalypse movie due to the wear and tear. Oh wait. Anyway, nothing is wrong with the mechanicals. Plus, the dents, dirt, and bloodstains give it some added character.

More than just idling, the wonderful Hemi engine simmers and seethes at rest, which is a great match for my mood. I get back in, click the autodown switches for both windows (over Jack's protests), put my seatbelt on, run up the revolutions per minute, and then suddenly dump the clutch. We take off in a shriek of rubber as the traction control fights with the monstrous torque of the V8 engine. Smoke pours out of the rear-tire wheel wells, and I work to keep the front end of the car pointing straight down the fairly narrow street. Jack grasps madly for the seatbelt and clicks it into place. He holds tight to the door handle, pushing back in his seat away from the asphalt being rapidly consumed under the hood of the car. Right as we near the red line on the tach, I stab the clutch to the floor and then drop it again, twitching the rear end of the car sideways for a second until the tires regain their grip. We howl through the neighborhood, the engine singing its wonderful song of pistons firing and burning gasoline. As we approach the exit to the development, I downshift into second as the stop sign for the main road comes into view.

"Stop sign, stop sign, stop sign!" Jack screeches.

I laugh as we go right through it (of course) in a cloud of rubber smoke, draping dual black marks across the pavement as the rear tires once again fight for grip. Accelerating down the street, shifting upward, and roughly dropping the clutch each time to provoke a firm chirp of the Goodyears, I glory in the brute power of the car and feel my pulse quicken as the speedometer races toward eighty miles per hour. In a forty-mile-per-hour zone.

I can hear the CD I've been playing recently and think it's perfect for the moment. Air Supply! No, nothing soothing—it's the magical, angry audio assault of Tool. Whatever has pissed them off, they have stayed angry their entire career. The wild tempo of bass, drums, and guitar thuds out of the speakers to mesh with the blast of the exhaust as we tear down the country roads.

The interstate is about three miles from the house, and the southbound lanes leading to Charlotte are clear all the way to the city. They're mostly empty thanks to doomsday—I've used the truck to remove the rest of the derelict cars over the past months. I've had a *lot* of free time after all, and driving is something that has always given me peace, all the way back to my teenage years. I especially love it at night when I'm just cruising, listening to music, feeling the solid car surrounding me, and gobbling the miles under the stars. We get to the highway in a hurry. I hammer the fast pedal as I turn left onto the entrance ramp and wind the engine toward the red line in second and then third gear. I watch the speedometer sweep to eighty. I bang into fourth gear and chase 100 miles per hour in a big hurry. I center the car on the white lane stripes, and the car devours them like Pac-Man on speed.

"So, where was the line drawn, Jack? Twelve? Eleven? You sick bastard."

"What are you talking about?" he sputters.

"You know what I'm talking about. I heard *everything* you said to that poor girl. The lying, manipulating a child, and pointing the finger at the rest of us so you could get your rocks off." I spit out the words. Even when angry, I'm still watching the road carefully. At this speed, I'm very aware that if something comes out onto the road—for example, one of the ever-multiplying deer who have no real predators any longer—we will be nothing more than red smears and car confetti strewn across the asphalt.

He says nothing, just sits there in silence looking out the passenger window at the trees blurring by. What's there to say? He's given me all the ammo I need to get rid of him and he knows it. He just doesn't know what's going to happen next. Neither do I, but I have an idea brewing. I say nothing either. I want to let him stew and worry. Silence is one of the greatest weapons in the world after all.

We sprint south toward the city just fifteen miles away, passing 120 miles per hour with the hot, spring wind pounding into the cabin of the car and buffeting us around. I pull my sunglasses down from their compartment above to keep my overlong hair from whipping into my eyes. I watch the needle pass 130 and see Jack shrink farther back into his seat if that's even possible.

The car feels like it has endless legs. I wonder what the top speed is and whether Dodge has put a governor on it to prevent their customers from creating bad press by invoking Darwin's rules. No matter, we're going ridiculously fast, and all the landmarks I have passed over the years of commuting fly by at nearly twice what I usually managed during rush hour. The car howls happily along, doing what a nasty muscle car is supposed to do—haul ass. Six minutes to the city!

I slow as we get to the outskirts, scanning either side of the highway for what I'm looking for. Seeing it off one of the exits, I pull the car onto surface roads. The engine settles into a softer growl as we creep at a more reasonable pace until we come to an intersection in the midst of one of the run-down sections of town. I can see a handful of zombies walking the streets in every direction, meandering in that aimless way they have when there's no food immediately in front of them. None are closer than a couple hundred yards away, which is perfect for what I have in mind. I notice one tottering on a nearby sidewalk, wearing a single shoe, a classy glass-soled high heel that may be three inches tall. Her clothes, or what's left of them, are skimpy and revealing, with all her assets (and frontsets) on display. Part of me is fascinated at the idea of her walking around for literally months on a single shoe. She probably has a stunning backache if they notice such things. Oddly, and I'm surprised to notice this, I feel bad for her—to be trapped in a mindless body and take no notice of anything other than an endless hunger. The other part of me takes note of her as a target and marks her distance and speed, just in case.

Setting the parking brake and leaving the car running, I slide the pistol out from between the seat and door and stick it in his face.

"Get out."

"What? Why? What are we doing here?" he asks, eyes darting around quickly as if trying to watch all the zombies at once. I suspect he's never had to fight and kill one before. He's probably just been hiding all along.

"Get. The. Fuck. Out."

He scrabbles to find the door handle, keeping his eyes on the barrel of the pistol, which probably looks the size of a beer can to him. We get out of the car at the same time, with me keeping the gun leveled at him over the roof of the car, taking care not to scratch the paint. A man's car is important to him after all.

"You have three choices, douchebag. One, I shoot you right now and get it all over with. I'll just tell the women we ran into too many zombies for us to handle ourselves and you didn't make it. I might even make you a hero, saying you sacrificed yourself to save me. Two, I leave you here to fend for yourself. Maybe I'll leave you a gun. Oh look! They've seen us or smelled or heard us. And they're all minorities! I bet you're a piece-of-shit racist too, or do you draw the line at trying to screw kids?" And they *have* seen, smelled, or heard us, as several of them have turned and are making their way toward the car, shrinking the distance steadily. They're now within about 100 yards or so.

As if on cue, I hear the first *Muuuuuuuhhhhh!*

"Three, you get your shit together and decide to be part of the solution instead of part of the problem. There are five of us. Five. Against who-knows-how-many of them. We have to stick together and work as a team if we want to have any chance of surviving. You, my friend, are not helping in that regard, and I was tired of your crap even before today. You just talked a fourteen-year-old girl into having sex with you, not to make babies for those monsters but to satisfy whatever it is that's wrong with you. Think about that— fourteen goddamn years old! Convince me I shouldn't leave you here right now. You won't last thirty seconds."

He speaks quickly. "No! Don't leave, don't shoot. I'll be good, I swear! I don't know what came over me with Amelie. I'm scared and angry all the time. You all hate me, especially you and Eve. I'm not tough like you are, and I don't know what to do. I just wanted … " He trails off, and I watch him carefully, knowing he's no dummy and suspecting this is an act of self-preservation.

Muuuuuuuhhhhh! Within fifty yards. I wait.

"I'm sorry," he blubbers. "I feel useless. You always seem to know what to do, how to build the walls, find food and water, fight them, except you haven't figured out how to get rid of the ones in the neighborhood. Why don't you just blow them up or something? Or why don't we all leave like you've been talking about?" All his words come out in a rush as his head swivels to watch in every direction. Since I'm getting a little distracted by the very close zombies and the possibility that we're going to have to fight our way out of here, I almost miss the second-to-last sentence. As I replay it in my head, combined with something he said weeks ago, the elusive thought finally clicks into place. For all of his faults, Jack has given me an idea. A wonderful, awful idea.

I'm not going to shoot or leave him (not today, anyway), but I want to make sure he has the fear of God (or me) firmly in him. "Get in."

I settle back into the car quickly and disengage the brake. He gets in, too, and straps his seatbelt on right away. The nearest zombies are within ten yards on all sides of the car. I push the gearshift over to the right and up into reverse and drill the gas pedal as I release the clutch. The one immediately behind us goes down with a wet thump. Then I switch into first gear and floor it. One more bumps off the passenger door, splattering Jack with blood as the side mirror gouges a divot in its midsection. He splutters and curses, madly wiping the mess off his face. I watch the zombie hooker step from a nearby curb, nearly fall into the street due to her lopsided footwear, and then gather herself. The yawning mess of her mouth groans open as we pass by. I resist the urge to deposit a bullet in her as we do so.

We accelerate away and head back toward the highway for home in total silence other than the song of the Challenger's exhaust singing its sweet, howling notes.

CHAPTER 19

I let him go into the house first while I sit in the car and think. He's still going to be a problem, of that I have no doubt, but he's likely to be more well-behaved for some time. From now on, he obviously can't be left alone with any of the women.

Eve comes to the door after a few minutes and waves at me, ushering me inside. I get out and pause next to her on the stoop. She gives a slight smile and then hugs me close. It feels nice.

"That was the right thing to do. We talked to Amelie, and I think she understands and believes us. She was scared, or 'grossed out' in her words, but was going to go through with it because she believed what he said about us wanting them to have sex. She's used to doing what adults tell her, like most kids. She's been doing that with us, too, now that I realize it. We've given her instructions on everything. Like, Go find water in that house. Grab those cans of food from the grocery store. Don't play with guns. Well, do play with guns. But, she kind of drifts on the fringes of our group—too young to really fit in with us but old enough to understand almost everything. I'm glad we don't have to try and explain that you killed him. That would have been difficult to sell." Her voice is muffled with her face pressed against my chest. Since she doesn't really touch me when she comes in for sleepovers—we just sleep back-to-back—this more personal contact feels comforting and more connected.

"Okay, good. We need to watch him now more than ever. I don't trust him. Though, I think I put a good scare into him, so he should behave. But he's going to be sneakier, so we can't take our eyes off him."

"Yeah" is all she says, which is enough.

I go inside and start looking through the kitchen drawers and cabinets. DeeDee comes into the room and watches me for a minute.

"Whatcha looking for?" she finally asks.

"Of all things, the yellow pages. When was the last time anyone actually used those instead of the internet or their phone?" I reply.

"The yellow pages? For what?"

"Dynamite," I say with a grin as I find the book and page I want.

CHAPTER 20

From what I understand, dynamite was virtually impossible to get in the old days. It required identification, licensing, and payment in traceable form. Plus, all purchases were recorded and reported to assorted authorities. That was then and this is now. The place I find is back in south Charlotte, right near where Jack and I were having our "whose dick is bigger contest"— it's mine; I've seen him in his birthday suit after all. Frank's Construction & Demolition Wholesale Supplies & Video Rentals advertises that they carry all sorts of demolition accoutrements, including dynamite. The phone book is three years old (again, who used these?), so I hope they haven't gone out of business or cleared things out since then.

I call Eve and DeeDee to get their attention and explain what I'm planning. One of them will come with me, just so I'll have help and company, while the other will remain with Jack and Amelie to keep an eye (and gun) on things.

DeeDee turns to Eve and says she'll stay back because she'll have no hesitation in putting Jack down if needed. She also figures her body might distract him from Amelie. With that being settled, the three of us go tell the others. Then we all head out front to get ready for our departure.

They are there.

All of them.

Somehow, they arrived this time without us hearing them.

I hand one .45 handgun to Eve and the other one to DeeDee, who actually passes it to Amelie saying, "You know what to do, baby," before picking up the rifle. I lean in past her and pull the shotgun from the umbrella stand. Jack stands there weaponless, but that's fine with me. He is, however, extremely nervous, and I remember he has not been through this exercise in insanity.

We march down the driveway, me and the three women with Jack trailing. We go out through the gate and onto the street to face the zombie queen and her sidekicks. There are no humans with them this time. I wonder if they've completed all their searches through the neighborhood and surrounding areas. If so, then that means we are it. Five people and about fifty zombies in northern Charlotte suburbs—seems about right.

As before, the queen slides forward and stops in front of us. She's once again being flanked by her two mammoth louts. What were they before all this? Some kind of pro football team? Both of them are significantly bigger than me, easily six-four and two hundred fiftyish pounds. I try not to think of how they've managed to maintain their size. By contrast, she's compact and slight, though not tiny. From our side, Jack stands slightly behind me and to the left. The women are on my right: DeeDee, Amelie, and then Eve.

The queen comes forward and looks at me, no more than a step and a half away. I can smell her putrid essence wafting through the air, and I close my nose so I won't gag. She glances at Jack, then back to me. I shrug. *You're not in charge of all deliveries apparently.* Then she moves close to DeeDee and takes a deep, ragged breath through her nose. She shakes her head and stares at her, then me. She moves down the line, repeating the process. Finally, she comes back to me. More staring as she shakes her head in anger with her lips pulled back from her teeth. I notice one of her incisors is missing. She holds up four fingers.

"Four? Yeah, there are four of us, plus Jack, so you can kind of count," I say sarcastically. I'm sick of her bullshit, sick of this process, and sick of the horrible idea she has in mind. I'm just tired of everything. Part of me wonders if I can hand them Jack, and they'll be satisfied and go away. You know, like a peace offering. Or an appetizer.

She thrusts her hand with the four-fingered sign closer to my face. Then she gestures toward the sky, waving her arm in an arch from east to west. Then she points to each of the women in turn. I get it after a second.

"You're giving us four weeks for them to be pregnant?"

She shakes her head, her hair raggedly swinging to obscure her face for a moment, and waves her arm in an arch once, twice, thrice, and then a fourth time. Uh oh.

"Four *days*? Does that include today?"

A savage nod. Four days, or really less than that, for all three of the women to be pregnant and creating food for the queen of the monsters. Sure, it's possible—I'm not going to explain how since we don't have time for a scientific detour right now. But, if my idea pans out, it isn't going to be necessary to even consider beyond the sheer unthinkable notion.

"Sure thing. We'll get right on that. Come back in four days for another sniff," I say dismissively. I'm not sure if they can follow sarcasm or not, but my voice is certainly dripping with it.

Both of her zombie-man-monsters come forward and loom over me from either side of her. I'm not short, and it's rare for me to have to look up at people (or things), and I find I don't like it. The message is clear. Four days, three pregnant women, or full-scale war.

"Got it. Now, go away so we can get busy."

The three musketeers hover for a moment longer and then move away, back down the way they came. As we watch them leave, I hear Jack take in a breath and say, "What the ... "

For once, he has it right.

CHAPTER 21

This changes nothing other than it pushes the timing of things forward and spurs us to action. I'm still a little stumped about what to do once I have the dynamite, but I just figure I'll have to hurry up with that part of the planning while we're getting it.

After making sure the crowbar is in the car for the doors of the demo place, Eve and I get in and leave for Charlotte. It's a much more peaceful drive than the one I went on earlier. As we wind our way through the industrial-focused roads off the interstate on the way to our destination, Eve pipes up suddenly and snaps me out of my thoughts. I'm trying to solve all the problems: killing the monsters, keeping us all safe, getting rid of Jack in a polite way if possible, and getting the hell out of Dodge in one piece. Just mundane stuff like that.

"I lied. I lied when I told you I couldn't have children. I was afraid of them, afraid of you, at first. At least, I think I can have children. We never tried." She stops, thoughtfully looking out the window as we pass a convenience store.

She resumes. "Do you think we should do it? Get pregnant to buy more time? They won't do anything to us for nine months. Maybe, even if just one of us got pregnant, they'd leave us alone since it would be more than they have now. It would give you a lot of time to figure out how to kill them."

I think about that—the idea has some merit. Then, I also come to the realization that she's offering herself to me since I'm damn sure she isn't suggesting she's going to sleep with Jack. I don't know what to say. Other people might have been comfortable with a physical relationship without an emotional component, but that's not the way I'm wired. I care about all three women, mainly because they're my obligation to protect, and we've grown close in this crazy new world where we have to rely on one another for everything. My relationship with both of the adult women is fairly confusing—I have evening company at least three days a week. DeeDee is more physical about it, snuggling in close to me and practically wrapping herself around me. Eve has kept up the back-to-back routine, but she ensures contact throughout the night. I feel close to both of them, which is natural given what we're going through, but I've also been trying to prevent myself from developing any deeper feelings for both of them due to the situation, too, since that could confuse everything and everyone. I know I have to reply, but I'm not really prepared for this, so it'll probably come out awkward.

"I think you're probably right that they'd leave us alone if one of you was expecting, but what if you're not? What if they decided to take one of us as punishment? Or kill one of us to send a message to the rest? There's not much we could do to prevent it since we're out in the open for the smell test and terribly outnumbered. Aside from Jack, I don't want to risk anyone's safety. Plus, there's a chance she might view Jack as a more cooperative surrogate father. So, she might take or attack whoever is not pregnant, or she'll come after me since I appear to be calling the shots. They don't want to eliminate the food suppliers. I think it's a good idea but risky. Let's not throw anything out, but maybe let's save that one and talk later in case this doesn't work." I hope she doesn't take offense at the indirect answer, especially if she's feeling me out for anything here besides trying to solve a problem, but it also seems like something that will benefit from more thought and conversation.

After a few more minutes of searching, we find Frank's shop, park the car in the lot, and go up to the front doors. There's no indication of Video Rentals on the façade, but then I notice a now-dormant neon sign with the word "Videos" written in cursive. I can see one of the ubiquitous, standalone rental boxes inside the front door. I have a hard time following why someone would swing by the dynamite shop just to pick up a movie for the weekend, but then again, construction work in Charlotte has slowed in the past few years just as it has elsewhere in the country. Maybe he added it for a little extra income.

The doors are a pretty typical pair of glass doors, and I'm surprised at that. Why just glass front doors when there are high explosives inside? I find out quickly after just tossing the crowbar through the right-hand doorframe and letting the glass tumble to the ground. We ease under the jagged stalactites still dangling and get to a service desk where we're stopped dead in the water. Behind the raised countertop, past a picture pinned to a corkboard of a guy I assume is Frank, there's a series of steel bars worthy of Leavenworth.

Based on his picture, I can tell Frank is in his middle thirties, with a Mohawk, and definitely looks like a guy who likes to blow stuff up. He's also clearly a guy who doesn't want someone else to take his dynamite and blow stuff up without his permission. Exposed I-beams in the ceiling are the top anchors, and the bars disappear into the cold, poured-concrete floor and run across the width of the building.

Not a problem, I hope. There's got to be a key around here somewhere. But after we clamber over the counter and get a better look at the lock, my hopes sink. It's a mechanical lock with five raised buttons arranged vertically on the left side under a small, twist knob. We tear the front area apart looking for the code, hoping for a scrap of paper taped under the keyboard or inside a drawer. No luck. We punch in a bunch of random combinations, but without knowing how many characters are in the code, it's essentially a waste of time. I look at the picture of Frank and silently curse him for being the right amount of paranoid for this line of business. We're screwed.

Discouraged, we climb back over the counter and out to the Challenger, dragging our feet as we walk to the car. I foolishly only noted this one place carrying demolition supplies. There are probably others in the phone book, but I left it at home. Perhaps we can find one in a nearby store since we didn't stumble across one while we were code hunting.

I drive us slowly out of the lot, pondering what we're going to do next and whether Eve's idea on the drive down is our only recourse. No way are all three women getting pregnant in the next few days. I admit, I'm out of ideas.

At least, I am until we pass a sign for Richie G's Refuse & Hauling Services just past the All That Beauty Salon on the right-hand side. I slam on the brakes and back up until we're parallel with the driveway into the lot. Eve mumbles a "What the hell?" but I just point out her passenger window. There are three enormous dump trucks sitting outside their fence. That's all the "key" we're going to need.

This time, we find keys inside hanging on a pegboard on the wall near the service counter. We match the first key to a truck; I try to start it, but the engine refuses to turn over, the battery weakly conking out after a few turns of the ignition. I repeat the attempt on the next one without success. The third one looks brand new—flawless except for a few months of dust and may have a fresher battery. Fingers crossed, I twist the key and it turns over after a few cranks. I've never driven a dump truck before, but I have driven stick my whole life, so I'm not worried about getting it moving. I let it idle for a couple minutes to make sure it won't stall after the months of inactivity, then I drive back toward Frank's with Eve trailing in the Challenger. As I check the rearview mirror, I notice how tiny she looks sitting in the driver's seat.

I pull into the lot on the side of the building next to Frank's. Visually measuring where I think the bars are, I back the truck as far away as I can and then floor it. There are roughly 150 feet between the buildings, with one curb and a couple-foot-wide median in the middle, then a chain-link fence topped with razor wire to negotiate. Of course, that won't be a problem for a vehicle of this size. Frank may have good security measures, but I'm sure the huge assault dump truck never made it into the possible scenarios of how someone might try to break in.

The truck hits the curb at about fifteen miles an hour and hops just enough to bash my head on the roof of the cab. I manage to hang on to the steering wheel and keep accelerating. I catch a peripheral glimpse of Eve leaning against the car and then turn back to the chalky, gray-painted cinder block wall in front of the truck. I snug my seatbelt on quickly and pull it tight, gripping the steering wheel as firmly as I can. The wall rushes toward me, filling my vision. I close my eyes and duck my head just before the truck explodes into the side of the building. It comes to a stuttering halt about eight feet inside and then stalls. Shards of block clunk off the roof and hood of the truck, falling to the floor amid the clouds of dust billowing into the back of Frank's. I feel something on my head and reach up to find a trickle of blood making its way down my temple. Nothing serious, so I climb down from the cab and find the crates of dynamite—nicely labeled and organized—right in the middle of the floor on a wooden pallet. Eve comes to the new "door" and calls in to ask if I'm all right. I say I am, then grab a crate and hoist it onto my shoulder and move through the gap left by the truck.

"How much do you think we need?" she asks.

"No clue," I reply. "Everything I know about dynamite I've learned from movies and books, so let's assume I know nothing and just bring a bunch. My guess is that it's probably better to have more than you need than not enough, so let's take this whole box."

We load the crate into the car, go back inside, and find what looks like about a mile of supplemental fuse cord, which will be more than enough to experiment with for timing. I pat our "key" as we walk past the front fender and head back to Huntersville and home.

We're running out of daylight by the time we get home. Rather than bring the explosives into the house, we drive to a house a few doors down—just to be on the safe side—and set them inside the garage. No one's going to steal them, after all, but why take a chance and have them inside our house? Once we get home, DeeDee reports that all has been quiet since we left, with both Jack and Amelie buried in books in the waning light.

CHAPTER 22

For a change, I have no visitors that night. Eve's feelings may have been stung by my not-too-subtle rejection in the car, or it just may be time for a solo night. I'm not great at reading women and never have been. No reason to assume I'd get better at it when the world came crashing down. In any regard, sleep is slow in coming as I wonder what exactly I should do with the dynamite. My basic idea is to carefully bring it over to their cul-de-sac during the day and leave it in the street. Then, I'll light it at night remotely with a long fuse when they all gather for their hunting routines. But given that these zombies seem smarter than your average zombies (for whatever that's worth), they may notice a giant pile of dynamite sitting in the middle of the street. Without any kind of background on what dynamite does in the real world when it explodes—as opposed to the varying carnage it wrought in movies and such—I can't be sure a pile of it is going to get them all, especially since much of the force of the explosion may go vertically.

I relax and let my mind wander on its varying routes rather than focus on the immediate problem. Hopefully, an idea will come if I'm not directly trying to solve it. This has been a good technique for me when trying to sort through abstract-feeling problems. I'm not always a quick-decision, immediate-course-of-action kind of guy. I'm more of an analytical, figure-it-out-at-the-right-pace kind of guy. Thinking back to all the movies I've seen over the years where explosives were prevalent (especially in war movies), I try to replay how they have been used. Finally, I bump into the concept of Claymore mines. Those have been in many movies, and from what I've followed, the explosive is behind a bunch of shrapnel that can be pointed toward the target. When detonated, the shrapnel is shaped to where the mine has been aimed and utterly wipes out the enemy in a nasty hail of death and dismemberment. No way am I going to find a Claymore—I have no clue where you'd even start looking—but the idea brings me back to an old childhood memory.

In the days before M-80 firecrackers were outlawed (or at least more difficult to get), one of my buddies had come up with a similar idea. In the amazing stupidity that can come with male adolescence, a group of us gathered at his house in the backyard to watch. His "bomb" was a paper cup filled with BBs surrounding an M-80. The rest of us were hidden behind trees in the yard while Jerry ran in, lit the fuse, and then ran like hell to dive behind a wheelbarrow. The result was spectacular and as advertised—the M-80 went off with a wonderful bang, BBs whizzed in every direction, including into the sliding glass doors not fifteen feet away. Needless to say, when Jerry's parents got home, he was in deep shit.

We didn't see him for several weeks. That wasn't the last of his pyrotechnic ideas, but it connected the dots for me as to how I'm going to exterminate a crapload of zombies at once.

I spend the morning of the next day experimenting with lengths of fuse and lighting them with an ancient Zippo I found in the dresser in my bedroom. Seems Jack's buddy David likes to smoke a little weed or cigars or cigarettes. It takes me a while, but I finally find a lighter fluid can in the garage and fill the Zippo up. My watch has a stopwatch, so we keep cutting pieces, lighting them, and measuring the time to burn until we have the feet-per-second equation figured out. Now, we need to go hunting, but that's going to have to wait for tonight. I have an errand to run in the meantime, thanks to the idea my old pyromaniac friend gave me last night.

Off to Home Depot I go, alone this time. The doors are still ajar from my many prior visits. I carefully sweep the aisles to ensure I'm alone before finding one of the flat-bottomed dolly carts and heading to the building materials section. It only takes a few minutes to find what I'm looking for—roofing nails, which come loose in thirty-pound boxes or in coils for nail guns. The labels claim there are seven thousand nails per box. Who had the crappy job of counting nails? I load ten boxes onto the dolly then make my way through the checkout area and out to the car. Three hundred pounds of nails fit just fine in the trunk of the Challenger. I go back inside and head toward the moving and storage section to gather packing peanuts. My plan is to load the dynamite into one of the rolling trash cans provided for each house—one each for recyclables, trash, and landscape waste—and surround it with the nails. However, the can will be monstrously heavy and difficult to move fully loaded with nails, so I'm going to dilute it to some extent with packing peanuts so nails are in place from top to bottom.

Back to the house, where we unload the car and set about creating the zombie bomb. After clearing out a horrible-smelling trash can from one of the neighboring houses—which apparently had an infant in it beforehand because there was a reeking mass of several-months-ripe dirty diapers in said trash can—we put a milk crate upside down on the bottom of the can to roughly center the explosives, wind the fuses together on a dozen sticks of the dynamite, and then mix nails and peanuts up to the brim. I punch a hole in the top with a screwdriver and hammer and thread the master fuse through it. Without knowing exactly how much of a fuse line we'll need—I'll have to find a place where I'll be able to see the zombies but also be far enough out of range—I coil 500 feet of it on top of the can. I don't think that will be enough to avoid any of the projectiles, but I also plan to light the fuse and then run like hell.

"Jack, where is your old house? Can we walk to it wheeling the trash can?" I ask.

He thinks for a minute and then shakes his head. "We kind of can, but there is no direct, short route from here that's paved. We'd have to go the long way on Cherokee Lane, over to Onondaga Way, and then finally to Blackfoot Court."

I know what he's talking about; it's one of my jogging routes that gives me a five-mile circuit up and down hills and through much of the development. It's what I like to call my "over-the-river-and-through-the-woods-past-grandma's-house" workout. So, we're faced with a two-and-a-half-mile distance, hauling close to three hundred pounds in an awkward trash can intended mostly to roll the length of a suburban driveway and little more. Lovely. I'm going to need help. The day had begun mildly enough with a cool breeze drifting across the golf course as I'd been sitting with my coffee, but it's now a searing-hot spring day complete with high humidity. We all eat lunch together—Chef Boyardee to the rescue—then Jack and I set out. I bring both pistols and the shotgun, though I don't give anything to Jack.

We don't talk much as we go, but he calls out dozens of his friends' houses he visited in the past. I realize he knows an enormous number of people in the neighborhood, while I only know two or three of the houses because they belong to old friends. It occurs to me that Jack has had his nice, cozy, American dream ripped out from under him—no matter how superficial I think his life may have been—and I feel a little sorry for him and myself.

For him, I guess the version of the world that was technology-obsessed, material-focused, back-slapping (and stabbing), consumptive, and wasteful had been just fine. I, however, had resisted it along the way and had as little to do with it as possible. It was fine if other people wanted to spend their days with their noses in their smartphones, but I preferred doing actual things, like running, playing golf, building things out of wood, working in my yard. Tangible things. Watching a video of someone else playing a video game seemed like utter insanity to me, and yet I knew kids did that a lot. So, I'd stuck with old rules like being polite and considerate, stopping at stop signs, being candid and honest, and being selective about my (small) circle of friends. Which, as a result, had left me comfortably alone most of the time, kind of like how I was before the women and Jack arrived. Granted, my transition to the new reality has been less bumpy than his thanks to my solitary style and hands-on preferences, but perhaps his prior life had been more enjoyable (to him) than mine had been (to me).

He's still an asshole.

Yes, yes he is. But I feel a little more sympathy for the devil and mentally decide to try and be more forgiving.

By the time we arrive, we're both pouring sweat. The shotgun has chafed my right shoulder blade nearly raw from rubbing against my sweaty shirt as we marched through the neighborhood, alternating who had the trash can. Whoever had been on the can pushed and pulled while the other scouted the surroundings, mostly for the rogue zombies, in particular. I know they're still out there, and I don't want to run into them since that will make for some noise. This needs to be quiet time. Both of us had to shove the trash can up the hills since the ungainly thing is just too heavy for one driver and handles something like a drunken rhino.

We stop around the corner of the entrance to Jack's old cul-de-sac. After waiting five full minutes to ensure nothing is creeping around, we walk the can down the street, strolling like we're taking a walk in the park and nothing is going on. I figure our truce with the queen and her friends has us covered, but we've never come visiting before. I want to make sure none of them are around and she isn't here to control the minions. We don't want a massive firefight on our hands. They are zombies after all, and we're food.

All is quiet on Blackfoot Court. The abrupt end to the world is as evident here as it is throughout the neighborhood, with children's bikes resting askew, lawns and shrubs growing unruly in the quickening spring, and scattered lawn tools rusting on driveways and front walks, waiting for long-gone hands to put them back where they belong.

We can't put the trash can right smack in the middle of the street—that will just endanger the plan—so we set it off to one side fairly close to a handful of other cans out waiting for a trash pickup that will never come. I assume a dozen sticks of dynamite and two hundred-plus pounds or so of nails are going to be sufficient for the job regardless of placement. We scan the area one more time and then head back toward our house in a different direction than we came now that we aren't burdened by the trash can. Unwinding the fuse as we go between two houses—one of them his, he points out smugly since it's massive—through a backyard and over a wrought iron fence, we make our way to the top of a small hillock that overlooks the back of his house and gives a clear view of the circle. There's ample wild shrubbery nearby to give us visual cover, and given the distance, I hope the zombies obviously enhanced sense of smell will not pick us up when we return.

The way back is through some of the woods bordering the development. The trees also screen the contemporary homes from the much older, original, ranch-style homes, whose owners had sold their adjacent family farmland to developers so they could turn it into a golf course and neighborhood. Of course, now it's a zombie breeding ground. I hope those families got a ton of money for the land. However, I suspect they received maybe a tenth of what the developer and builder turned around and charged the suburbanites who moved into the "country" to live with thousands of other people.

We have to fight our way through the undergrowth clawing at our sweaty shirts and clinging to the shotgun as I pass, but this cuts more than a mile off our trek. We make it back to the house around cocktail hour. I resist the desire for a strong drink to settle the nerves. They've been howling at me for the past three hours. But since tonight's going to be a late one, and I'm already exhausted from crappy sleep the prior night, I don't want to dull the edges in any way.

All of us gather in the family room to discuss tonight's dry run and set out the tasks we'll each have. Jack's going with me, mainly because I don't want to chance that, if everything goes to hell and I get caught or killed, he'll end up being the women's only hope for protection. This way, if I go down, he's coming with me, and they'll at least be safe from him if not the remaining zombies. The women will finish packing the truck this evening and have it parked right at the base of the driveway, ready to go at a moment's notice. We don't expect anything to happen tonight, but if it does, the plan is for them to leave the area right away since all-out war with the zombies is likely, and the fortress wall is never going to keep all of them out. We agree that if Jack and I are not back within two hours from leaving, they're to leave the house and go to the nearby shopping center. It has a giant sprawl of parking lot that will provide a clear field of vision and fire. They'll wait there another hour. If neither of us join them, they're to leave for Pennsylvania. Eve has family there and knows the way. Everyone is tense. I try to soften the mood and keep everyone loose, but I have little success. The next two nights are going to change everything, no matter how they turn out.

CHAPTER 23

Against my better judgment, I give Jack a pistol as we head into the gloom of the night at nine o'clock sharp. It was one thing to leave him unarmed before, but we're going to head through the dark, into their environment, and go right to where they're living and patrolling or whatever it is they do. He has never handled a gun before except for the video game pistols his children had, so I give him a quick lesson on how to handle one. If we're discovered, two pistols, a shotgun, and the KNIFE—remember, Australian accent at all times—are going to buy us some time but not our lives. I don't bring this fact to Jack's attention. If we get in trouble, I may just shoot him immediately in order to spare him—and get my gun back quickly.

The temperature and humidity are still high, unseasonably so, as we tramp off down the street to make our way to the partial path through the woods. A waning moon has crept over the horizon to silhouette the blooming trees in monochrome fashion. I smell the sweetly septic odor of the Bradford pear trees that are (for some reason) so popular here. They're one of the earliest blooming flora in spring and are attractive trees, but their blooms smell like a zombie's butt. Not that I've smelled zombie ass.

It takes us far longer than I expected, and I wonder if the two-hour plan for the women to depart is going to backfire on us. The moon throws insufficient light for us to see clearly, especially once we're under tree cover and shrouded even further despite the few, early leaves unfolding from their buds. It's about a mile and a half to Jack's street going this way, and what took us about thirty-five minutes earlier is going to be nearly double that in the dark. We stop and freeze at every single noise in the undergrowth, waiting to confirm it's nothing predatory, and as we get closer and closer to our destination, I feel us slowing as we work to minimize the noise we're making.

I have no clue if the zombies post sentries or something, but Jack told me he had seen nothing the first time he witnessed their evening ritual. We finally make it, fifty-eight minutes after we left according to the glow of my watch. Super—we have ten minutes or so to see what we've come to see and then hightail it back before the women leave. At least we can jog on the return trip once we get clear of the woods, so the final three quarters of a mile will be quick. Especially if we're being chased.

We silently get on our hands and knees for the last 100 yards, creeping forward like two kids who are playing army in the woods and are sneaking up to rain water balloons on unsuspecting girls lying out in the sun. As we near our overlook spot on the hill behind the homes, we see the moon break out from the passing clouds, making our trash can visible. I find the tree where we tied the fuse off the ground and wrapped a white plastic bag to a branch so we'd be able to locate it in the darkness. We sink to the ground amid the smell of fallen leaves giving back to their Mother.

Surrounding their leader dead-center in the cul-de-sac is what looks like the entire horde of monsters, awaiting instructions for the evening's festivities. Just like Jack described, she's waving at small groups of them and then gesturing in various directions, to which they depart. I decide we'll have to come at least fifteen minutes earlier for the real run tomorrow night to be able to get them all. I'm fascinated by the silent, grotesque ballet she's coordinating and almost don't hear Jack shuffle to his feet after a couple minutes.

"I have to piss," he whispers.

"Are you kidding me?" I hiss back. "Now? You couldn't have gone at the house or along the way?" I feel like a parent scolding his kid for waiting fifteen minutes after going on a road trip before declaring they have to go potty.

"Yes! Look, I'm scared by all of this commando shit and those fifty goddamn zombies down there who'd just as soon eat us as go find different food," he replies quietly but with vehemence.

There's no point in making him hold it, though part of me takes a second to decide whether to tell him to suck it up. I nod my assent and he moves back through the woods and into the shadows, out of the grasp of the moonlight. I have to hand it to him—he moves quietly.

I turn back onto my stomach to watch the zombies move around the street below us. More than half of them have been dispatched by now, and those who remain are no more than thirty feet from our zombie-buster bomb.

This is going to work as long as we get here early enough, and they gather every night at the same time.

I feel more than hear Jack's return a couple minutes after he departed. I expect him to come down next to me and watch until it's time to go. We have fifty minutes to make it back before the girls will leave the house. If they do, then we'll have one hour to jog another three miles or so in order to meet them at the backup rendezvous point. Not really a problem since jogging three miles in an hour is a joke, but if anyone gets hurt or turns an ankle in a deadfall in the woods, all bets are off.

When he doesn't lie back down, I raise up on an elbow and turn back to where I know he's standing. "Jack," I whisper as I turn. "What're you doing?"

As I make it all the way around and see him, I freeze. He's standing above me with his pistol drawn—though turned sideways, movie-gangster style—and from what I can tell, not quite aimed at me. That being said, I feel my insides go cold, my balls constrict, and maybe a little pee sneaks out. Adrenaline flushes through my body out of anger at myself for giving him the gun and fear that this piece of shit is going to kill or wound me, and therefore, screw up the escape. I think of the women being confined by this deviant bastard, especially Amelie, forced to create food for the monsters and satisfy his urges. I'm furious, but I'm also on the wrong end of the gun. I keep still.

"What are you doing?" I repeat. "This isn't going to solve anything. I know you have a beef with me, and that's fair, but this is going to get both of us killed and I don't think you want to be zombie chow." Or so I hope.

"Shut up. I hate you," he spits. "Drop the guns, both of them. You make me look bad in front of the women. You think you're so smart and able to solve everything. Well, I'm intelligent and capable too. More than you know. It was me who gave you the idea to blow them up after all. I'm going to kill you and then go back to the women and tell them *you* were the hero and saved me—thanks for the idea, smart guy. Then, it'll be all about Jack. *My* rules, *my* women." The moon lights his face. While he may look nervous, and the pistol is shaking a bit in his hand, he also looks serious. I push the .45 handgun off to the side and settle the shotgun into the leaf beds on my right, making sure he can see me do so. I'm shaking a good bit myself.

"No, Jack, you're totally right," I say soothingly while thinking quickly. "You *are* smart, and I haven't been fair to you. It was a really good idea to make the bomb. And see, you got the drop on me. But if you kill me here, they're going to hear it and come see what's going on," I add, gesturing back toward the group still remaining in the street. "And they'll be able to see the muzzle flash and find you easily. Some of them are out there already, too, and *she* has some way of communicating with them without words. Some of

them might be diverted to get between you and the house."
He starts to look less sure of himself.

"Let's go. We've seen what we came to see. We'll talk
tomorrow about how to make things better between us.
We'll get Eve and DeeDee to talk, too, so all the grownups
can get on the same page," I say as I rise slowly to my feet,
arms at my sides so he can see my hands are empty.

I estimate the distance between us at six feet and confirm
his aim is a little off-center. I can't afford to get hit at all,
and I don't like that we're so close. It will be difficult for him
to miss without taking at least some piece of meat off me.
Thinking back to when we went over the gun, I recall how
I went over the safety with him, but I can't remember if I
switched it on before turning the gun over. I'm sure I did, so
if he has forgotten to remove it, he's in for a surprise. If he
has remembered, then I better be damn fast and lucky.

As we have been talking, I have gradually lowered my
stance and spread my feet out to shoulder width in order
to move rapidly sideways and then at him when the time
is right. I'm going to take the gun from him, but after that
I'm not sure. Everything I've just said applies to me too—
if I shoot him here, they'll see and come hunting. Not to
mention, I'll be taking the chance it will ruin the plans for
tomorrow evening. I still have the KNIFE, but that is likely
to be noisy too. And, I admit to myself, I haven't killed a
non-zombie by hand, and I still have some hesitation about
killing one of the last humans, even one I vehemently dislike.

I'm not afraid, but I don't want to die. The fear of
death is clearer now after the End. Before that, it was an

intangible thing, something that would happen way down the road. But in these days, I'm aware it's something that could happen at any moment, which made for a pretty rude reality check. All that has happened has shown me what a tenuous grip we all have on this thing called life, and everything that has occurred since then has made me value what is left of it even more than I did before. I think of Eve snuggling against me at night and sleeping in the comfort of my company. I think of DeeDee coming out from the changing room in her naughty outfit with a huge grin on her face—*and let's not forget that view of the twins.* I think of Amelie's need for her oddball collection of surrogate parents to watch over her. I think of my own desire to protect all of them and go find what we can of our families. As fucked up as the world has become, as much as fear chases us every day and can wear on us like nothing in the past ever could, I'm damned attached to sticking around and taking care of my people.

He's thinking, staring over my shoulder while doing so, though the gun never wavers from its aim. His gaze clears, and I know he has come to a decision. "You know, you're right. I can't kill you here," he says. "Let's move it." He gestures with the pistol, twitching it toward himself, but gives me no window.

"You go first. Leave the guns," he continues. "I can come back for them another time."

I figure he's going to kill me somewhere on the way back to the house, far enough away from where we are to avoid discovery and close enough to the house to race home in case of any of the patrolling critters. That eliminates the woods, where it will be too difficult to run, and leaves out the last half mile or so out of the woods. My guess is that shortly after we make it into the regular streets of the neighborhood, he'll pull the trigger.

I rack my brain, thinking of how to disarm him beforehand. *Should I trip over an unseen branch and then pop up and attack him? Should I run wildly through the woods and hope he won't or can't hit me?* Both ideas seem like they'll work.

I keep planning as we move quietly through the trees, pushing our way silently through the shrubbery. From time to time, he jabs me in the back with the pistol, mumbling to himself about "Jack's rules" and other unintelligible mutterings. Abruptly, we clear the tree line, and I realize I have missed my chance as we step into the unblocked moonlight. Jack pushes me harder than before with the gun, not a poke but a shove to separate us, and tells me to stop.

"Are you too chicken to shoot me from the front, Jack? Don't want to look me in the face before you pull the trigger?" I ask, trying to buy a few more moments, but my brain isn't helping me—I'm out of ideas other than trying to just dive to the side and hope for the best.

"No," he whines, drawing the word out. "Fine then, turn around. Let's get this over with." He sounds shaky, and I'm hoping that will give me at least a split second of extra time.

As I turn, madly thinking about fake-tripping or something, I hear a branch snap from behind him. A pretty big branch. He hears it, too, and we both freeze like garden statues. A shuffle of leaves follows, and then another smaller branch cracks, though it sounds like a sonic boom in the silence.

Muuuuuuuhhhhh!

Oh shit.

Jack spins around to face where we'd exited the trees. It's a single zombie, though a big one, looming out of the woods, right back the way we came. Jack's between it and me, no more than twenty yards separating them.

"Shoot it! Shoot it, Jack!" I shout.

The zombie has obviously seen us and is accelerating across the grass of the common area we're standing in. Their run isn't pretty, but they move at something close to a slow jog by our standards. The space is closing quickly as Jack raises the pistol, screams a shrill "Die!" and squeezes the trigger.

Nothing. Dipshit has indeed left the safety on the whole time. I could have taken the gun from him at any moment. I'm furious for lots of reasons but first, I'm moving.

As Jack fumbles with the pistol, I cross the two steps to him and rip the gun from his hands. I thumb the safety off and rack the slide on the gun to chamber a round. The zombie is still a few steps away, arms raised and closing in on us, when I shoot it in the chest. It staggers to the side but keeps its feet. I step closer and put the second round through its forehead. I don't even bother to watch it fall before I turn back to Jack.

I slam the pistol against the side of his head. He goes down with a cry, holding his right hand to his bleeding temple, and looks up at me helplessly.

"You asshole!" I seethe with anger and aim the gun at his face. My hand is shaking, but that's just from the raw adrenaline drag racing through my body. I'm going to end this once and for all since he's finally given me the perfect excuse to do so.

Don't.

What do you mean, don't? He was five seconds away from killing me! The only thing that saved me was a goddamn zombie of all things. He's a dead man. I'm shooting him and maybe not to kill with the first bullet either.

No. There is a better way. Perhaps a more sporting way.

And then the voice tells me an old joke. I nod to myself, lower the gun, and tell Jack to get moving. We jog back to the house, not a word between us along the way, until we get to our street.

"You're not sleeping in the house tonight. No way. I don't care where you go, but when we get back, you tell everyone you're sleeping elsewhere."

He looks at me for a minute, but there's nothing to say, no argument to make, and he knows it. He nods in assent, and we continue up the hill to the house.

We make it back just as the women are getting into the truck. We haven't made it back inside the two hours, but once they heard the gunshots, they decided to give us an extra fifteen minutes in case we needed help. DeeDee tells me she knew the shots were close by and figured that things hadn't gone haywire since there were only two shots—if she'd heard a bunch of shots, then she was going to take the other two away. Smart woman.

I say nothing of what happened between me and Jack. I only mention the attack from a single zombie and how Jack tumbled during the melee, hence the scrape on his head. I explain that what Jack had described about their nocturnal activities is true and that we're going to push tomorrow's agenda forward fifteen minutes.

As we settle down, Jack says to the others that he's going to sleep in one of the other houses. If this is his last night alive, then he's going to sleep in a real bed instead of on the damn sofa. Good idea, Jack; atta boy.

I hand him a flashlight so he can find his way, and he actually has the balls to ask me for a gun. It's all I can do to not laugh hysterically. I just look at him for a few moments, saying nothing. After a bit, he lowers his gaze and leaves. I go to the front door and watch him descend the driveway and go through the gate, locking it behind him. He flicks the flashlight on, casts it around at the houses in the cul-de-sac, and settles on one directly across the street. I watch him go, waiting for a light to come on in the house like you would in the past when dropping someone off for the evening, and then go back inside to the women once I remember that most of the old habits are toast like nearly everything else.

We all go to bed. Maybe some of us sleep, but I lie awake staring at the ceiling fan for a long time before dropping fitfully into the Sandman's embrace. I dream of a peaceful round of golf with Eve, DeeDee caddying.

CHAPTER 24

The next day is like a day at work after Thanksgiving. No one is in the office, there's little to do, and as a result, you can do whatever you want but it takes forever. Minutes drag; every glance at my watch shows that less than half the time I think has passed actually has.

Jack slinks around the house, avoiding me and never making eye contact. I'm sure he's a mix of happy for not being shot but also wary of why not. I was partly surprised this morning when he came back across the street, looking disheveled from what certainly had been a restless night. My guess is that I had been right—Jack has survived by hiding, not fighting, and knows his best chances for survival lie with the group.

The women shuffle around the house, doing this and that, but we're all on edge as we wait for nightfall. We go over the plan a few times, but really, it's a simple plan. We just do it to burn some time. We check through the supplies (again), make sure the truck is full of gas (again), find the backup weapons I store in my closet to replace those I left in the woods (thank *you*, Jack), which I plan on recouping tonight. I have the second .45 handgun, the KNIFE, and the rifle. I give another rifle to DeeDee, a nice little .38 revolver to Eve, and a compact .22 rifle to Amelie.

Night finally comes, and we all eat some dinner. It's pretty quiet except for the *tink* of silverware against the bowls as we eat some tasteless soup. All of us, maybe even Amelie, are clearly heavy with our thoughts. Jack has an uncertain future in his mind since he knows he's crossed the line; he probably figures he's at least going to be expelled from our little tribe since I didn't kill him last night. DeeDee and Eve have to be pondering, like me, what the future holds if this doesn't work.

Our deadline is fast approaching, and no one is pregnant. I doubt we can get an extension from the zombie queen. In all likelihood, they'll overrun us, enjoy what food we provide, and move on to find others. We also have the unknown of what'll happen if this does work and we get them all. We've decided we're going to leave, if we can, and the wide world is a bigger mystery than it has ever been. The destination is New York, outside of the city in the suburbs. If that fails, we'll go up into the Catskill Mountains, out in the middle of absolutely nowhere, where my family has had land and a little clutch of cabins since the turn of the last century. We will stop in Pennsylvania to look for Eve's family too. While we might get all of them, the Charlotte area is, or I guess was, too densely populated to provide real sanctuary. So, we're going to take our chances on the road and hope to find family or at least safety.

Jack is coming with me again, but obviously there's no weapon for him this time. I'll have him lead until we get to our site, and then I'll pick up the shotgun and pistol from last night's recon. I may even jab him in the spine with the .45 just so he gets a taste of his own medicine. I tell him I'll need him to help me spot, and if we run into trouble along the way, especially from the rogue zombies, one of us has to go light the fuse and wipe out as many of the others as we can. He looks uncomfortable at the prospect of accompanying me again, but the look in my eyes tells him he has no choice in the matter.

Before we leave, we awkwardly stand around and then say something along the lines of goodbye and good luck. Amelie surprises me and comes in for a quick hug. I hope we'll get through this for her sake above all others. I have no idea what she's seen along the way these past months since she never speaks about it, but kids shouldn't have to deal with the things she may have experienced, even ones from this desensitized world. I don't know her well at all despite our close quarters. She's fairly quiet and stays with DeeDee or Eve all the time, but I feel more protective about her than anyone else since she's just a kid and relies on us for pretty much everything. Maybe that's how parenthood feels. Maybe I'll get to find out someday, but if this works the way we want it to, it sure as hell won't be the way the queen has in mind.

Eve quietly comes to me and says nothing. She just brushes her lips along one cheek and places her hand on the other one for a moment, eyes looking into mine. I hug her tight—she's the first woman to really keep me company after all—and murmur reassuring things as we separate.

DeeDee, as always, is more brazen. She kisses me full on the lips (no tongue, thank goodness) with her torso pushing firmly against me. "Y'all be careful out there," she says as she steps back. "Come back to us. We need you." I sure plan on it but just nod. I'm damn nervous since, if this goes wrong, it's going to go *very* wrong.

"Two hours," I remind them. "No sandbagging and giving us extra time—just go. If we're able, we'll join you at Target." I look at the faces of the women in turn, taking them all in for one last, mental snapshot.

"Like DeeDee said last night, if you hear a bunch of shooting, just go too. That means we're in deep shit. We should be able to outrun them over a long distance, so that'll be the plan. Plus, this way we'll know which place to go to without guessing. I'm relying on you to be where you're supposed to be. Lots of shots, go to Target. Just a few, stay here up until two hours and then go." The women look unhappy with this, but they all nod in agreement.

CHAPTER 25

Jack and I leave at 8:45 p.m. on the button and move at an easy jog until we come to the edge of the woods. The zombie from last night is ripening quickly in the warm weather, and the air is clouded with his stench as we hurry past and step into the gloom of the trees. Tonight isn't as clear as it was last night. Fat, white clouds scud across the face of the moon and obscure what little light it generates, but we know the way and negotiate the rough path fairly quickly. It's warmer than last night, too, and I feel the sweat trickle down my back. I'm anxious, though it's a simple idea: boom go the zombies, or we're in a shit storm.

We sidle up to our spot, locating the white plastic bag drifting lazily from the branch in the light breeze. I tell Jack to stop. I feel around for the pistol and shotgun and add them to my arsenal, tucking the .45 into the waistband of my pants and leaning the shotgun against a tree away from Jack.

There they all are, assembling in the darkness and meandering in their curious way into the center of the street from the nearby homes and yards. I wonder where, how, and if they sleep. *In beds? Out in the open? Standing up?* I can vaguely make out the queen and her two beasts in the midst of the gently bubbling mass of zombies.

No time like the present and nothing else to wait for. I unwind the fuse from the tree branch and let the bag drift away into the undergrowth like a handkerchief floating in the breeze in a romantic movie. Wriggling the Zippo from my pocket, I open it with the famous *clink* and smell the lighter fluid wafting up, raising childhood memories of my father lighting up a cigarette on our back porch that overlooked the small lake we grew up on. I transfer the lighter to my left hand before spinning the wheel. I turn to Jack as I start to stand up.

"Hey, Jack."

"What?"

"You know the old one about two guys getting chased by a bear?"

"What the hell are you talking about?" he asks, also starting to stand.

I slam the .45 into the side of his head, butt first, harder than last time, and then drop it at his feet. It may indeed be more sporting this way. He goes down like a sack of potatoes.

"You just have to be faster than the other guy."

I light the fuse and start to count, keeping an eye on Jack. He isn't moving much, and I'm worried I hit him harder than intended. At the end of the night, it isn't going to matter. When I get to one hundred, I raise the rifle and fire two shots into the gaggle of zombies below. Two bodies drop. The muzzle flash is bright, and I'm glad I remembered to keep one eye closed to retain my night vision. Fifty heads swivel toward me, and I see the queen wave her arms silently toward the hill and our overlook. Four zombies detach from the mob and begin to run toward us.

Jack starts to stir a little more, which is good, for him anyway. I take one last look at him, grab the shotgun, continue counting in my head, and tear off through the woods. The way away from our base on the hill is slightly downhill, so the crest will shield me from the explosion and the shrapnel, which should be coming in three … two …

The world pauses as if taking a deep breath. I hear the sound of my footsteps flattening leaves but nothing else, not even my breathing. I'm knocked loose from my pace as the earth bumps and heaves beneath my feet. I stumble to the ground. There's an enormous *KA-WHUMP* from over the edge of the hill, followed immediately by the loudest swarm of bees in history. It sounds like someone has thrown a massive pile of silverware onto a tile floor as the nails expand outward in a hail of death, colliding with bodies, cars, and houses. I turn to see the flame from the explosion licking its way to the sky, pushing an oily black cloud ahead of it. Screams—or whatever it is zombies do aside from that stupid *Muuuuuuuhhhhh!* sound—echo from the cul-de-sac.

Before turning away and running to the house, I spy three silhouettes reach the top of the hill where Jack should be lying. Shouts and gunfire follow immediately, but there are only two shots. I smile and then run and run.

I'm back well inside two hours, but I find the women waiting on the front porch. It was impossible to miss the explosion, and they've apparently heard all four shots. They've been debating whether that qualifies as a bunch or not.

"Where's Jack?" asks Eve.

"He didn't make it, or at least I don't think he did," I reply. "We ran into three zombies right after lighting the fuse, and they must have gotten him. He got a couple of shots off." None of that is a lie.

"Let's go. If any of them are still alive, they know where we are and are sure to make this their first stop. I don't think we should take off for our trip yet. We need to check around in the morning, make sure Jack's not still alive somewhere and none of them are still crawling around either."

We all pile into the truck, DeeDee driving, and drive away from the neighborhood and go up and down the highway all night. We alternate drivers—even Amelie since she has to learn, and the DMV is a blissfully extinct entity now. I drop to sleep at some point, exhausted once the adrenaline and excitement wears off. I wake to find us idling in the Target parking lot. Eve is at the wheel but dozing, and DeeDee is in the back row of seats curled up with Amelie like a pair of slumbering kittens. It's early, with the sun just creeping over the horizon behind the false front of the store to our east.

I rouse Eve and switch places with her. Nudging the truck into Drive, I wind through the shopping carts strewn across the parking lot and back toward the house. The girls all slowly come to, with DeeDee saying she'd kill for a giant, real, Dunkin' Donuts coffee with cream and sugar.

We stop near the natural area that leads to the woods. I tell the women to wait for me and lock the doors. I want to be sure, so I hustle through the miniature forest to reach the overlook, my head on a swivel since I know Jack missed at least one zombie. I find Jack's body lying facedown just a couple steps from where I left him. Part of his face is torn off. To his credit, there are two dead zombies sprawled nearby, one holding what looks like Jack's face in his hand. Yuck.

Taking the fallen pistol from his hand to match the one I already have, I walk to the top of the hill and look down. The morning sunlight is just reaching the street on this side, painting part of the utter devastation below in warm, early light. I'm blown away—though I guess not as much as they have been. There's a mammoth crater—about the size of a few minivans—in the middle of the street, blackened at the edges by the flames I saw last night. The cars that had encircled the cul-de-sac have been thrown onto their sides or into the adjacent yards. Bare trees stand like silent, dark sentinels in the front lawns. Several of them have been burned down to skeletal remnants, their hands reaching from the turf. Every piece of glass has been blown out of the windows of the houses, and shredded curtains waft in the breeze. It's an awesome sight to behold.

I climb down the hill, pistols at the ready but knowing I won't need them. The devastation is massive. As I reach the outer circle of the explosion's reach, I have to step carefully around all the zombie bits and pieces. None of them are alive, and while there's no way I can count them all given what little remain, I figure we got almost all of them. I scan the area, seeing nails embedded in *everything*—from the sheet metal of cars studded with nails from every angle, to a garden gnome askew on his side with a perfect nail right smack in the middle of his forehead, to mailboxes full of holes.

Something near Jack's old house catches my eye. Both the giant zombies are lying in a pile, backs peppered with hundreds of nails. It dawns on me that I haven't seen the queen. I'm suspicious, so I cautiously move over to them and poke the top one with the pistol. He doesn't move, but to be on the safe side—in case there is such a thing as zombie possum—I put a bullet in the back of his head and then roll him onto his side. The other one is below him, and I get the idea. Much of his body is covered in nails, too, but I repeat the process.

There she is. The queen is still alive. Although, from the looks of her, she won't be for long. Half her hair is burned off, exposing a blistered scalp. One foot is gone and she, too, is riddled with nails despite the efforts of her protectors to shield her. Black-red blood trickles from the corner of her mouth. She turns her head, wincing in the sunlight, and looks up at me.

I drop to my knees and straddle her chest, knowing there is no danger here, to me at least. I fix her with my eyes as I draw the KNIFE out and wave it in front of her ravaged face. Grasping the hilt in my right hand and resting the palm of my left against the back of the glimmering steel near the tip, I lower the blade to her neck.

"This is my kingdom." I make contact with her skin, drawing a rivulet of blood with the KNIFE's edge.

"I have all the power." I push the blade downward, leaning all of my weight over it.

"Killing you is all the glory I want." The finish takes a grunt to drive the blade down all the way to the scarred pavement below her neck. Her eyes darken and go dead.

I don't know what forever holds, but this is day one.